MW00476641

DEAD WRONG

A CREE BLUE PSYCHIC EYE MYSTERY

Kate Allenton

Copyright © 2017 Kate Allenton
All rights reserved.

The unauthorized reproduction or distribution of this copyrighted work is illegal. Criminal copyright infringement (including infringement without monetary gain) is investigated by the FBI and is punishable by up to 5 years in federal prison and a fine of $250,000.
Please purchase only authorize electronic editions and do not participate in, or encourage, the electronic piracy of Copyrighted materials. Your support of the author's rights is appreciated.
This book is a work of fiction. Names, character, places, and incidents are the products of the author's imagination or use fictitiously. Any resemblance to actual events, locals or persons, living or dead, is entirely coincidental.
All rights reserved. Except for use in any review, the reproduction or utilization of this work, in whole or in part, in any form by any electronic, mechanical or other means now known or hereafter invented, is forbidden without the written permission of the publisher.

Published by Coastal Escape Publishing

Discover other titles by Kate Allenton
At

http://www.kateallenton.com

Copyright © 2017 Kate Allenton

All rights reserved.

ISBN-13: 978-1-944237-45-5

DEAD WRONG

DEDICATION

For the real Cree in my life that keeps me laughing and grounded in all ways that matter.

DEAD WRONG

Chapter 1

No trace of my identity existed in the message, or so I hoped. My white-gloved hands allowed for no fingerprints. The moisture sponge I'd used to seal the flap was devoid of DNA. The letter inside and address on the front was typed. No one would ever prove I wrote this. My conscience was free and clear, or it would be in three days when the letter reached its destination.

"God speed," I whispered as I slid the envelope into the mail bin. I'd taken all the necessary precautions. I looked like a proper young lady going to Sunday tea. Only in the south could I get away with the clothes I was wearing, and no one thought twice. I'd chosen this dress on purpose, vintage and untraceable.

My wide-brimmed hat blocked the hot afternoon sun and did more than act as an accessory. It hid my identity. Head down; check. No hair color visible; check, check. I felt like a mixture between a villain with a secret plan and a superhero trying anonymously to save the world. I like to think I fell somewhere in between. The thought made me giggle despite my churning gut. It happened every time I mailed one of my *special* life-changing letters.

I headed back into the parking garage and slipped inside my Jeep before I took a deep, satisfying, calming breath. I'd gotten away with it again. I tossed the hat into the passenger seat.

My brunette hair cascaded down my shoulders, and I gave it a little tousle making it as frazzled as my nerves.

The daze that followed sitting quietly in my car was like a clearing out of the closet in my head, making space for new crazy energy to enter. A mental reboot for the next game changer I'd write.

I fumbled through my purse, grabbing my phone seconds before it rang. I always thought of it as a creepy benefit of being psychic, but I was beginning to think maybe I had more than one wire crossed. I probably had several. "Hello."

"Cree Blue, you had better be two seconds away from walking in this door."

I moved the phone several inches away from my ear as Charlotte's tirade continued. Her high-pitched angry tone was like shoving pencils up my nose into my brain. If I were a betting girl, I'd lay money she was related to the inventor of dog whistles, car alarms, and the one note that no one could ever seem to hit in the national anthem.

Charlotte was my business partner and best friend, and she often reserved that tone for times when I left her with the new hires in the kitchen or when she was destroying new computer viruses. She was versatile like that.

I was like the mastermind behind New Creations, recipe inventor extraordinaire. We were legendary in the culinary world, well, at least in our own minds. She worked on entrees, while I stuck with the sweet desserts, but the creations weren't the reason for her tone. I was late. It was the story of my life.

"Sorry, I had to mail the letter. It couldn't wait." I shoved the key into my ignition and started the Jeep, revving the engine to prove I was actually on my way.

"*The* letter?"

"Yep. It's gone. No way to get it back unless I break a few federal laws and pry the mail drop box back open."

"It wouldn't be the first time," she teased. "Well, we both know that one was time sensitive, so you're forgiven for making me deal with these lunatics. I'll give you ten minutes to get your ass here, or I'm going to have to hire you to connect with their dead carcasses after I beat the crap out of them for arguing about which new video game is better than the others."

"I'll be there in ten minutes." Charlotte's death threat was a new low. She was a techie. She could deal with gamers and computer nerds with her eyes closed.

"Don't get a ticket, but hurry."

"Flash them your boobs, and they'll be in shock until I get there." I pulled out of the parking garage. "Or make yourself a strong drink."

"Liquor, lots of liquor should work. I'm timing you."

I ended the call and tossed my phone into my purse. Flashes of different things were already entering my mind. That wasn't the unusual part.

Flashes came to me all the time; when I was walking through the grocery store or making dinner and even once mid climax. The explosion of information almost kept me in bed for an hour. I didn't have the heart to break it to my then boyfriend that it wasn't anything he'd done. I let him keep his little ego fantasies. I was sweet like that.

Generally, I could ignore the flashes without even trying, but the letter I'd just mailed had sent a vibrational shock of live electrical currents zipping up and down my spine like an elevator on speed. One day those currents would make me meltdown, but today wasn't that day. I still had work to do.

My business cards didn't read, *Psychic Medium*. I still hid in the closet to everyone but my immediate friends and family. I didn't spout that I had clairvoyant gifts. I originally hadn't wanted them. I never grew up seeing dead people and was never warned when someone might die. I was a normal kid, well, as normal as one can be calling out lottery numbers before the lady on TV. The day my father died changed everything. Ghosts, spirits, premonitions, all now bombarded the inner workings of my mind without any way to turn those images off.

I turned in beneath the Lady Blue Plantation's iron gate. Trees lined the drive, providing a canopy-like tunnel down memory lane emerging into the expansiveness of my ancestral home.

Charlotte stood out like a breath of sunshine on the porch, sipping an umbrella drink with her feet propped up on the southern antebellum railing. A look of relief stretched across her face when she spotted me. It was a shift in the energy, a happily anticipated welcome home. The sins of my tardiness would soon disappear like the liquor in her glass.

She slowly rose from her perch and had reached my Jeep by the time I stuck it into park and killed the ignition.

"I thought you'd never get here."

"Did you put the boys in timeout and tell them mommy needed a drink?" I asked, slipping out of the car. My gaze traveled to the ballroom window. Goosebumps covered my arms. The rush of adrenaline from mailing the letter was slowly subsiding. A new emerging apprehensive energy filled the air buzzing around me and through my body, tugging at me to hurry.

"I've been out here hiding." She grinned.

"Did they all show?"

"Not everyone. We still can't reach Winston."

"That's okay. We'll proceed without him. Send condolences and flowers from the group. His grandfather died."

"How..." Her question died off. "Never mind.

She knew better than most that I'd get visions, flashes, stuff I didn't even want to remotely know, and it was all shown to me, everything but the purpose and the plan for the direction of my own life.

Laughter and talking died down as I entered the ballroom. Each analyst returned to their computers, ready and willing to help in my crazy venture. We were changing lives working together. Each person made me better and more efficient.

Their fingers clicked away at the keyboard. Mission control was already up and running. The screens around the room illuminated blue, sitting dormant ready for the surprise images to pop up on the screen. Today was the day I'd been mentally preparing for. An active case I wasn't sure any of us would ever be able to un-see.

"Nice of you to join us." Jitters called out from across the room. His nickname suited him well. He was always hyped on coffee; his fingers on the keyboard were always lightning fast. There wasn't a clue or hint ever missed when he was working *Insight*.

Insight was a computer program and equipment designed by my science-loving father who'd made it a personal mission to prove to the world that the Blues weren't a bunch of lunatics. When I was plugged in, the visions in my head were transferred to the jumbotrons in living color like a connection through space and time, letting everyone in the room experience what I saw while tuned in.

I tried for an apologetic smile, but I'm sure it came off more as a kiss-my-ass kind of grin as I pulled my white gloves off and tossed them on one of the empty desks.

Doctor Stone stood in the middle of the room next to the reclining hospital-type bed. The machines that monitored my vitals were already turned on. The only thing he needed to proceed was his guinea pig.

We'd done this song and dance for the last three years. I had quit needing the instructions my father had left after the first few times. "Whenever you're ready."

"Thanks, Doc."

"Which file are we working today?" Charlotte asked as she slid behind a computer screen.

"Sam Render," I announced and watched as the others exchanged the same look they gave each other every time we played this game.

"His case is still active and in the news. Why aren't we working on a cold case?"

"Gut feeling." I winked at Jitters and headed to the locker to pull out the newest wrapped brown paper bag inside. "Everyone knows the drill?"

They all nodded. I kicked off my shoes before climbing up into the hospital bed, never once giving the guys a peek of my Wonder Woman underwear beneath my dress. Doc Stone covered me with a blanket before sliding the rubber cap-like helmet over my head. My windblown hair was about to be matted with jelly-like goop. The things I did for answers.

I let out a shaky breath as he held the injector that looked like a common caulking gun with the cold sticky substance inside. It reminded me of that gel they put on a pregnant women's belly before a sonogram to see the little baby inside. This was kind of the same thing. Everyone was about to see the crazy images in my head.

"You ready?"

"Always." I smiled and closed my eyes, bracing myself for the Antarctic chill soon to follow. One by one he filled the holes first with the goop and then with the probes. I looked like Medusa with all of the cables attached to my head. This entire system had been my father's baby. He'd had the whole thing running from our basement for years before he passed away when the secrets of the *Insight* program were shared with me.

"Video is rolling," Jitters called out, adjusting one of the cameras on me and another on the screens. It was his backup to his backup of the computer recording. He was kind of paranoid like that.

The doctor stepped back with his finger hovering near the switch. "Just say when."

"Light me up like a frat boy at his first keg party."

He flicked the switch, and within seconds, the screens in the room flickered to life. Brilliant flashes of colorful light entered my mind before settling into place like a picture being exposed in a dark room. First one, and then two, and then more. Images of everything I was thinking of in my mind filtered across the hanging screens like a homemade movie of my twisted thoughts. I was only looking for one image. The one that calmed my soul like no other; my father's face. It was always there in the recesses of my mind.

I tore open the brown package resting on my lap to find a sweatshirt inside. Small. Old. Torn. Blood-stained. Fingerprint residue from the police lab processing it for clues still clung to the surface. Little holes had been cut out, probably to check for DNA.

"All systems are a go. Session is in order," Charlotte called out.

"Case File 54 Sammy Render." My voice was loud echoing through the room as I leaned back into the pillow, clutching the clothing tight in my hands. I closed my eyes, letting the emotional energy from the sweatshirt meld and soak into my skin, invading my pores.

Annoyance.

Odd that it wasn't the typical fear. I shoved my own thoughts aside and embraced the essence, letting the feeling of annoyance coil down my spine as my heart raced with anticipation. I waited for the connection, wrapping it around me like a wet blanket. "Let's hunt."

Images flooded my mind. I was a silent witness. I always was.

Sammy Render was a short kid. If I had to guess, he was about the age of ten, blonde hair, cute, and rambunctious. He was in a crowded park, kicking soccer balls with a friend on a dark and cloudy day. The leaves on the trees danced in the wind. Thunder rumbled in the distance. A storm was coming. The energy was like a living, breathing thing. There were a dozen people around. Women sitting on park benches talking while their children played. It was a typical park. Monkey bars, swing sets, slides, and a large grassy knoll that backed up into woods where kids kicked balls around or played games. My energy was tethered to Sammy's in the grassy area. When I was in *Insight* and focused, I'd flash exactly to the energy where I needed to be in that moment and able to observe everything surrounding it.

"Are you ready for this?" a boy taller than Sammy called out. His sweaty black hair was slick to his head while he juggled a soccer ball with his feet. He popped the soccer ball high into the air, and when it started to descend, he jumped. His foot met the ball with a force that sent it flying high and hard over Sammy's head. It sailed straight into the swell of green trees and walking trails before it disappeared out of sight.

Annoyance made sense. I would have sent the little punk in after it.

"Aw, now why did you go and do that, Frankenstein?" Sammy yelled at his friend before jogging toward the woods. *Sammy called Frankie, Frankenstein.*

Thunder grew louder, and lightning crackled in the sky. One of the mothers on the bench called Frankie's name as Sammy cleared the treeline.

Frankenstein turned to run to his mom, glancing back only once to where Sammy had disappeared into the trees. I shook my head and followed in behind him, unsure I wanted to see what happened next.

Sammy was twenty feet up an oak tree where the soccer ball was lodged between two branches. He was lying against one of the thick branches, shimmying out to the smaller branches that extended out like fingers on a palm.

I wanted to catch him. I wanted to scream that he needed to get his butt out of that tree. Hell, if I'd been there, I would have offered to replace the ball with ten more. Heights weren't my friend. It made me dizzy just watching with my feet firmly on the ground.

He swung and missed. The crackling of the branches was loud to my ears.

"He's going to fall." I covered my mouth with my hand as he swung again. He missed. The pops of the branches filled the silence. He and the branches were falling with the grace of an eighty-pound boulder toward the ground.

I cringed for impact, squeezing the sweatshirt tighter in my grasp.

Sammy landed with a thud on the broken branches. The tip of one was sticking out of his shoulder, soaking the fabric with blood around the wound. He yanked the branch free. A guttural cry of pain sprang from his lips as uncontrollable sobs filled the air.

I squatted next to him. The need to comfort him was overwhelming. I tried to rest my hand on his arm, knowing neither of us would feel the connection.

Sammy struggled out of his sweatshirt, tossing it aside and tore open the shirt beneath to examine the jagged open wound. The blood was flowing faster. Sammy's face paled, and his head lolled from side to side seconds before his eyes rolled back and lids fluttered shut. His body went limp, and he fell over.

The news reports mentioned searchers combing the woods when looking for him. The only trace they'd found was his bloody sweatshirt and the broken branches on the ground.

I'd known going into this that Sammy was still alive. My spirit guides had told me so. The community feared the worst, and in a way, I did too. Whoever had taken Sammy hadn't come forward yet. While their hope was fading after weeks of searching, I was looking for a living, breathing, scared-to-death little boy, and I wouldn't stop until I found him.

My dad's face flashed in my mind. He smiled triumphantly like he had the day I graduated college.

Doc Stone's gentle but firm voice filled my ears. "Stay focused on Sammy, Cree. You aren't done yet."

It was hard not to grasp the image of my father and hold it forever. The ache in my chest clenched tighter until tears slid down my cheek. "Sorry, Dad," I whispered and returned my gaze to Sammy.

A woman was with him now. One I didn't recognize. She lifted him in her arms and was carrying him away. I followed behind, trying my best to get a good look at her face so it would show on the screen. She kept her eyes down on Sammy. Her words were soft in the wind. "I've got you."

She placed an unconscious Sammy into the back of her car before jogging around to the driver's side. She glanced up and down the street before sliding behind the wheel. I walked to the back of the car for the license plate, getting a good look at the local tag before I whispered, "You may have him now, but not for long, you won't."

My eyes popped open in a panic, like being woken from a scary dream. My entire body was trembling as Doc Stone piled more blankets over my body to warm my freezing body core. It always turned cold when I did this work. The longer I was tuned in, the worse it would get. Doc Stone monitored my vitals, his fingers resting on my pulse while staring at his watch. He'd only ever had to yank me out once before.

"Tell me you got that." My whisper was barely audible in the quiet room when Charlotte reached my side.

"We got her."

"I'm piecing out the other images that popped into your mind into another file so Sammy will be one continuous feed," Jitter's called out.

I relaxed into the warmth of the blankets, closing my eyes as my heartbeat calmed. My energy was zapped; my dream state was fast approaching while the others did what they do best.

My usual recovery time was about an hour. This time it was three. Shadows from the windows danced on the ballroom floor. The sun was shining in through the west windows as I slowly pushed myself up on the bed. Doctor Stone was the only one in the darkened room, reading a newspaper while sitting in a chair.

"You were out longer this time," he said, folding the paper in his hands.

"I didn't sleep well last night," I said, throwing the blankets off my legs. "Did everyone leave?"

He nodded and patted the sweatshirt with a paper sitting on top. "I kicked them out so you could get some sleep, but they left what you need to take to the police."

I slid out of bed, wiping the sleep from my eyes. "Thanks, Doc."

"I'll show myself out. I know you need to get changed."

Within the hour I was up and showered and dressed in jeans and a T-shirt heading out the door with the package containing the bloody sweatshirt and the paper with the license plate number. That little boy needed to come home, and I was his only conduit to make it happen.

Chapter 2

Only one man in law enforcement knew how my family and *Insight* worked. Daddy thought it wise to keep it that way, and I was never one to question his decision.

There were three working mediums in a fifty-mile radius, not counting those still in the closet, but none of them had *Insight* technology. No one did.

There were a million ways Big Brother could use it on criminals and prisoners of war, and that was never part of my father's intention.

The Billson Police Department was only a twenty-minute drive away from the Lady Blue. Our Mississippi community wasn't large nor was it small. We bordered on the knowing the neighbors in our own particular neighborhood but when people ventured outside those boundaries, there were too many people to get to know. That was another reason I traveled across town to mail my letters.

Sally Carbine grinned at me from behind the bulletproof glass as I approached. Her police badge shined and sparkled like her bubbly personality. Sally was somewhat like me. She wasn't like a typical cop. Sure, she had a badge and a gun and probably the training to put me on my butt, but Sally was more of a behind-the-scenes kind of girl. She always greeted everyone with a smile on her face like the seedy world of criminals and mayhem couldn't touch her behind the bulletproof glass plate.

I didn't work with Sally. I'm pretty sure she didn't even know what I did. Detective John Faraday was the man. He was my go-to guy and one of my father's oldest friends, not to mention my godfather.

We had a symbiotic relationship. He gave me the packages, and I helped him find answers once cases turned cold.

"Is Faraday in?"

The smile on Sally's face slipped as she shook her head. She pointed toward the side door and buzzed me into the restricted area. "You haven't heard?"

"Did he retire and forget to tell me?" I folded my arms on the counter and glanced around the quiet cubicles, which were usually buzzing with activity.

"He was brutally attacked and shot in a home invasion last night. He's at County General."

"You're joking, right?" I asked, standing straighter. No way I could believe someone got the drop on Faraday. He was too smart and too clever to ever become a statistic.

"I'm sorry, Cree. This isn't a joke. There was a break in one of his cases and we couldn't reach him so another officer drove out to his house and thank god he did. He probably saved his life. Faraday could have bled out and died."

My mouth parted, and my heart seized. I wasn't prepared for this. No, this wasn't supposed to happen. I was psychic for God sake. What good was I if I couldn't keep the people closest to me safe? "Is he going to live?"

"He made it through surgery. That's all I know."

I closed my eyes and peered beyond the veil in search of answers and was only met with silence. I hated silence; it was like a chill on a cold winter's day.

Sally's warm palm rested on my arm. Her voice turned serious, threaded with concern. "Are you okay?"

I lifted my gaze and swallowed around the lump in my throat. "I'm fine."

"Can someone else help you, or were you just here for a social visit?"

Her question reminded me I still had important information to share. It was just a question of who might believe me. A little boy's life hung in the balance, so I shoved all worry aside. "Who's working the Sammy Render case?"

"Detective Mason Spencer took over that case. Would you like to talk to him?"

Yes, no, crap. I chewed my bottom lip. How was I going to explain this without divulging my secret? It was too time sensitive to call it into the tip line. Would he even believe me? Today was as good a day as any to be locked away in a straight jacket that secured in the back. Did they let a person make calls from the psych ward? I was about to find out. "Yes, please."

Damn. Trepidation swarmed in my gut. Heat covered my body from my head to my toes. I slipped out of my jacket and fanned myself as Sally spoke quietly on the phone. "She works with Faraday." I heard her say at the same time I noticed one of the officers rise from his seat behind his cubicle wall. He raised his brow while staring at me with the phone held to his ear.

This had disaster written all over it. I straightened my shoulders and wiggled my fingers watching as he hung up the phone. I watched his every move, his every irritated facial expression as he approached. His dark hair was messy like he'd just run his fingers through it. His dark blue eyes were calculating. Tattoos peeked beneath the arm cuffs of the t-shirt stretched across his chest. He was the epitome of how I pictured detectives on TV; seductively bad ass and as lethal as the gun at his hip.

"Detective Mason Spencer, this is Cree Blue."

My guides whispered his real first name, making me grin. I guess if there was any time to go balls to the wall to convince these people, I might as well use every card I'm given. "Nice to meet you, Leonard."

His brows dipped, and his no-nonsense penetrating gaze turned to a glare. "No one calls me by Leonard but my grandmother. I go by middle name, Mason. How did you know that?"

I leaned in and whispered. "I'm psychic. It's a gift, which brings me to why I'm here."

"Great." Mason's annoyance seeped in that one word, instantly telling me what my guides had neglected to say. Mason was a damn skeptic. Just peachy. I had one shot to get this right. One shot to convince him that I was playing with a full deck and he should follow through on what I was about to tell him. I pulled at the hem of my T-shirt, only now wishing I'd worn a business suit.

He motioned toward one of the interrogation rooms. "If you'll follow me."

Walking into the room, I took a seat in one of the cold, hard metal chairs. The vibe in the air was one of confusion and regret mixed with the sour taste of anger. "You should really consider clearing the energy out of this room. You might get a better response when you ask questions. I could bring you some sage to try."

His jaw ticked. The muscles in his arm bunched as he studied me, not taking me up on my offer to help.

"Fine. You can't say I didn't offer." An old rotary-style phone sat at the end of the table. A two-way mirror hung on one of the walls. The light on the video mic was thankfully turned off, and it would be his word against mine. At least I could call my lawyer. I slid the package to the other vacant seat.

"Ms. Blue. Let me start by saying—"

'You're a skeptic. I get it," I answered for him. "You aren't the first." I gave him that sugary-sweet smile that I'd perfected just for people like him. "I actually thought of just turning around and leaving, but the information I have is kind of time sensitive. So just humor me, please."

He crossed his arms over his chest and remained standing. "What can we do for you?"

I gestured toward the package and waited for him to open it. His frown deepened, as did the color of his blue eyes when he noticed what was inside the package. "Where did you get this? It's the missing evidence."

"It wasn't missing. Please sit. You're giving me a crick in my neck." I gestured for him to sit and didn't continue until he did. "Faraday gave it to me." I held up my hand to stop an argument I could see rattling in that brain of his. Mason Spencer wasn't a man to fly off the handle. I could read it in his energy, the way he remained silent, using as few words as possible to get to the truth. Every word out of his mouth was thought about and planned. He took his job seriously. He was tall, intimidating, and observant. "After your lab processed it of course."

His eyes narrowed. "That's against protocol."

"Be glad he did." I cleared my throat. "I generally help Faraday off the record with cold cases. I don't do it for money or recognition. I do it to help. If I can even find one new lead, the family might be closer to having some closure. Since he's in the hospital, you'll have to do."

"Okay, I'll bite." He moved his hand in a circular motion, wanting me to move things along.

"First, I want to make a deal."

His tight glare relaxed. "Immunity?"

"Funny." Not. This guy was like a double shot of hard bourbon, and I was a glass of sweet tea. The two would never mix well, kind of like a weekend drunk and Monday morning staff meeting conducted by a room full of nuns. "If the information I give you results in finding Sammy, I want access to Faraday's house."

"Can't do it. That's an active case, not to mention a closed crime scene."

"Semantics. I can help you figure out who hurt Faraday."

"You aren't a cop."

I leaned back in my chair, crossing my arms over my chest. "I never claimed to be, but you strike me as smarter than the average badge. Let me help you. What's the worst that can happen? You already think I'm a fraud."

"You think the information you have is worth me just letting you waltz in on our investigation."

I nodded. "I have information that will lead you straight to Sammy, and not only that but a living, breathing hurt little boy that was taken from the woods. That Sammy."

His eye twitched. The skepticism stretched across his face. Seconds ticked by before his lips tilted into a grin. "You give me the kid, and I find out you had something to do with this, I'm going to enjoy locking you away."

I rose from my seat. "I'll give you the *missing link* you need to find the kid, and an unbreakable alibi. I want access to Faraday's home."

"Fine." He crossed his arms and leaned back in his seat as if waiting to watch me fail.

"The kid fell from the tree." I pointed to the hole. "He landed on a branch that stuck him. He passed out, and a woman came along and took him."

"Is that it?" He rose from his spot. "Is that your best guess?"

I took the piece of paper with the license plate number out of my pocket and slid it across the table to him. "She has shoulder-length brown curly hair. The car she was driving was a four-door Chrysler. You'll find his blood in the backseat where she laid him.

When she took him, he was wounded but still alive."

He picked up the license plate number and glanced at it. "For all I know, this plate number belongs to someone you hate."

I took a business card out of my pocket and set it in front of him. "If that's the case, you'll know where to find me. Try to prove I'm wrong."

I walked over to the door and pulled it open, turning around with my hand on the knob. "Sammy has a nickname for Frankie, the kid he was playing soccer with in the park. He called him Frankenstein when the ball got kicked in the trees. If you don't believe me, ask the kid." I pointed to the license plate. "Sammy's alive, and you're wasting precious time. Do your damn job, Mason, Leonard, whatever you like to call yourself. Take the win. Go get that kid and take him home to his devastated family."

Chapter 3

After leaving the police station, I headed straight for the hospital to visit John, only to be turned away by the police officers guarding his door. Only family was allowed to see him, which was ironic since I was the only family he had, even if we weren't blood-related.

It didn't take long for the news to break. Sammy Render found alive, and his kidnapper was being booked in the county jail. I wasn't one to gloat... much.

I picked up the phone and dialed the precinct, asking for Detective Spencer. He answered on the first ring.

"This is Spencer."

"Mason, this is Cree Blue."

He let out an audible sigh, but even that wouldn't deter me.

"Congratulations on finding the kid."

"Thanks." He cleared his throat. "Listen, I talked to Faraday today."

"They wouldn't let me in to see him. How is he?"

"He's tough. He's already out of the woods, but I told him about Render and that you wanted to go to his house."

"He said no, didn't he? He's worried I'll be exposed."

"How do you know that?"

"The same way I know you don't have any leads on who did this to him." I sighed. "I'm already exposed. I crossed that bridge when I came out of the closet to you."

"Cree, he doesn't want you in on the investigation."

Of course, he didn't. He was stubborn to a fault and cared about me like my own dad would. It was the main reason why he only brought me cold cases. "You know I can help you figure this out. I've already proven myself, and we had a deal."

I got that ringing feeling again, only it wasn't my phone about to ring. It was his.

"I'll wait. You need to answer that call."

"What call...."

The phone rang as if I'd planned the whole thing out and was calling on another line.

I waited impatiently for him to return.

"I'm back. Where were we?"

His voice sounded somewhat frazzled, his mind obviously elsewhere and not on our conversation. "Was that an important call?"

"You tell me, and if you get it right, then I'll take you to Faraday's."

I sighed and closed my eyes, asking my guides for the intel. Their answer made me smile. "The FBI called you to set up an interview. Congratulations again."

"Okay fine, but if we're going to do this, we're going to do it my way. I'll pick you up at seven tomorrow night."

"Why not in the morning? Don't you want to get a jump on this?"

"My way, Cree, or not at all. Take it or leave it."

"I'll take it. Oh, and I need one more favor."

"I can't wait to hear this one."

"Get me on the approved list to visit Faraday."

"That's easy enough. He's lucid. I'll tell him you want to see him."

"Thanks. Now go celebrate, Mason. The FBI is going to be lucky to have you. I have it on good authority you're a shoo-in."

I left him speechless as I hung up the phone. Nervous energy coiled around me. My sleep wasn't going to be easy tonight when I needed it the most. Going to Faraday's house was important. I could feel it in my bones down to my soul.

Tomorrow I'd have to stay busy, or I'd be crawling out of my skin in anticipation, and there was only one way that helped me keep my mind preoccupied. Tomorrow was going to be another cooking day.

Chapter 4

The doorbell chimed through the house, and I took a glimpse at my watch. "Crap."

My kitchen was in shambles as workers scurried about. The aroma of fresh-baked cookies filled the air as I wiped my hands on my apron. "Charlotte, you got this?"

She rolled her eyes. I knew the answer without having to ask.

I grabbed two cookies that had been cooling and took a bite out of one as I answered the door.

Mason was waiting on my stoop with a garment bag strung over his arm. I shoved the other cookie into his mouth, and he had no choice but to bite.

"Too chocolaty?" I asked as I pulled the door open wide.

"Mmmm," he answered, swallowing hard as he shoved the rest of the cookie into his mouth. "It's perfect."

"It's a keeper," I yelled toward the kitchen as I led Detective Spencer into the library.

"Did I catch you at a bad time?" he asked.

"No, sorry. I was working on a new recipe, and time slipped away from me." I untied the apron and pulled it from around my neck. "I'm ready; just let me grab my purse."

He handed me the garment bag. "We're doing this my way."

"Of course," I said and glanced, a bit perplexed, at the bag.

"Faraday is worried about your safety and shielding your identity. So go change. I'll wait here."

"Is this necessary?"

"If you don't want to do time for B&E."

I wasn't used to being ordered around, but if whatever he'd brought could get me into the crime scene to help my friend, I wouldn't question it. Not yet. The jail was not a place I wanted to call home.

I jogged up the stairs and into my room, dropping the bag onto my bed. I unzipped the contents to find a police uniform encased in the bag. The name read *Officer Sally Carbine*.

"Interesting." Sally and I weren't even the same sizes, and I had suspicions that this uniform wasn't a one-size-fits-all kind of outfit.

Men. I sighed and slipped out of my clothes and put on the scratchy uniform. Everything about this outfit screamed hell no. The pants were three inches too long. The buttons on the top tugged to contain my breast, leaving a gap. I slipped into my heeled boots to keep the material from dragging on the ground.

Yanking at the collar, I headed back downstairs to find Mason no longer in the library. Instead, Charlotte and he had moved to the ballroom.

"We use the computers and monitors when Cree does her charity auctions. She was making sure everything still works."

Thank God, the rest of the equipment had been squirreled away. "I don't know how you guys wear this uniform. It's itchy and ungiving and definitely doesn't compliment a woman's figure."

They both turned to me. Charlotte hid her smile behind her hand. Mason's gaze slowly slid down my body and back up until he met my face. He cleared his throat and gave me a ponytail holder. "You need to put your hair up the way you girls do in that messy pile on top of your head." He then held out a pair of oversized sunglasses. "And put these on too."

"Seriously?" I asked, twirling my hair up into a messy bun.

"The point is to hide your identity. We aren't leaving here until I'm satisfied you won't be recognized."

I took the sunglasses and slid them on my face before holding out my hands. I looked like a hot mess. I could see it in Charlotte's grin. "Does this work?"

"You look like a hot stripper cop heading to work a bachelor party," Charlotte answered, earning my glare.

I sighed. If we didn't come up with something and fast, I had a feeling Mason was close to calling the whole thing off and changing his mind. My eyes widened, and I grinned.

"Don't move." I held up my palms. "Give me five minutes to change."

I ran up the stairs, unbuttoning my top as I hit the landing, and ran toward the end of the hall. I threw open my grandmother's door. Her signature perfume smacked me in the face as I headed for her closet. I pulled down one of her favorite dresses and slid it over my head. The material hung on my body like an oversized tent. I took a pillow and slid it beneath, using one of Grammy's belts to hold it in place. I padded my bra with toilet paper to make my rack appear on the larger side before slipping Grammy's favorite wig on my head. I was studying my appearance in the mirror when I spotted her reading glasses with the chain. I slipped those on too and rested the readers on my nose. Grammy's energy swirled around me, cocooning me inside a sense of calm and peace. This was going to work, or we might never know the truth.

I changed into her practical pumps and had to stuff those to make them fit before grabbing her cane. I hunched over and headed down the stairs into the ballroom.

"How do I look, sonny?" I imitated my Grammy's voice. I'd had years of practice mimicking her as she scolded me.

Charlotte burst into laughter.

Mason's eyes widened in horror.

"You're a younger version of Grammy but without the wrinkles," Charlotte announced as she walked around me, glancing at my chest. "My, what big boobs you have."

"I'm not Red Riding Hood, and you aren't the big bad perverted wolf."

She chuckled. "I never would have guessed you could pull off the old lady."

Mason grunted and headed for the door. "Let's go."

He pulled open the door to find Jitters standing on the stoop. His gaze went past Mason's to mine, and the color drained from his face. He took an unconscious step back as we walked out with Charlotte behind us.

"Grammy Blue?" His words were a whisper, and I grinned without breaking character. I took my time down the steps with the use of my cane. "Don't tell me that Cree has also figured a way to raise the dead."

Charlotte took Jitters by the hand and pulled him into the house as I made it to the SUV. She called out, "Have her back before curfew."

"You must resemble your grandmother."

I grinned as I fought the cane, stabbing it into the floorboard.

He took it from me and gently laid it so that it would rest against the center console. "Thanks. If you were to see pictures of both of us at my age, people would have thought we were sisters, if not twins."

He nodded and turned around in the drive, heading out onto the highway.

"I was almost certain you weren't going to take me. What changed your mind?"

"When I told Faraday about you wanting to go to his house, he said that you'd just end up breaking in."

That was probably true, although I'd been a little concerned about anyone who might help getting into trouble too.

"Did you tell his guards to give me access?"

"Of course, I said I would." Mason turned quiet with his eyes on the road until he glanced my way out of the corner of his eye. "So have you been like….that your whole life?"

"You mean sexy cop stripper or southern grandma?" I grinned.

He gave me a sideways smirk.

"Oh, you're talking about dead people and knowing things. No, not my whole life," I answered, turning my gaze to the window. "If I had to describe it, it was like someone one day decided, hey, let's screw with her, and flicked a switch and bam. I knew things without asking and was just blurting them out."

"Like lottery numbers?"

I lolled my head in his direction. "Something like that, although I'd never play the numbers. It might kill my karma if I did."

"Karma." He grunted. Cops seldom believed in things they couldn't explain. That was why I'd never wear a badge. I believed in the impossible growing up listening to legendary tales from Grammy and my dad how they helped people in a different kind of way. The kind of way that couldn't be proved or seen with the naked eye. I didn't give much thought into how it all worked or why, only that it did.

"Imagine knowing something about every person you meet. Most of the time I try to shield myself from the incoming messages. I never try to overstep my bounds."

"I find that hard to believe," he said, pulling into Faraday's drive.

Crime scene tape stretched around the house and through the trees. A sense of foreboding filled my veins as if my body knew exactly what had happened behind those walls.

Don't go in. A stoplight flashed in my head. Instead of the yellow, green and red, it was filled with all red and flashing. I shoved the uneasy feeling aside and climbed out of the car. I'd gotten this far. No way was I turning around now.

"You good?" Mason asked as he waited in front of the car.

I used my cane, taking my time as Mason let his gaze scan the wooded area. He ushered me by the elbow up to the porch stairs and raised the tape for me to pass before using a key to unlock the door.

"So how does this work if there isn't a dead person?"

I shrugged. I'd never worked a crime scene. "I work with the energy from items. If it's highly charged energy, then I can usually get images and potentially more with the help of my guides. Sometimes it's like a movie. Other times, I'm not so lucky."

I stepped into the darkened house. The curtains and blinds were open across the room, bathing moonlight across the small dining room table. The only other light came from the laundry room that led to the garage.

"Go to town," Mason said.

The chair facing the television held a lot of energy. Every time I stopped by to visit on Faraday's days off, I often found him sitting in it and drinking a beer. It was a mixture of Faraday's hard-nose energy and something much more sinister.

I stood behind it and inhaled, calming my churning stomach. Blood covered the cushions, arms, and some of the headrest, making my stomach churn as the smell assaulted my nose. The hair on my neck prickled, as did the energy that was drawing me to touch it. I closed my eyes and opened the veil. That was the place where I like to think the information I shouldn't know came from. A high-pitched hum started in my ears as I reached out to touch the chair.

Visions slid into my mind in quick succession. "There were three."

I let out a shaky breath and continued. "He was hit from behind." I was getting woozy from the angry energy. My legs felt like noodles. I dropped to a crouch without breaking the connection. "A baseball bat." I pointed toward the floor. "He was bleeding from his head." I touched the back of mine to show where. "Oh, God, no."

"What?" Mason asked.

"They have a gun to his head. His eyes are open. He's looking directly at the masked man."

"What are they saying, Blue?"

"Give us a name," I repeated over and over again and watched in horror as they beat Faraday. "They're hitting him because he won't answer."

A tear rolled down my cheek, the scene to unbearable to watch, but I forced myself to stay in the moment. "They lifted his head by his hair. Blood gurgled from his lips. 'Who told you about Moreno's gun, and where did you get it?' The guy is yelling at him…"

"Talk to me, Cree. What are they doing?"

I shook my head as if trying to un-see the brutality. "Faraday spat blood from his mouth and told them to go to hell."

"He shoved Faraday's head back against the floor and stood over him with the gun." My heart raced in response, and when the guy pulled the trigger twice, it made me jump. "They shot him twice; once in the chest, the other missed and hit his arm."

"Give me a description, Blue. What are they wearing? Hair color, eyes, anything."

"They're all wearing black with ski masks, and they're about your height and build," I answered, unable to take my eyes off Faraday. I held out a hand to where he lay as if to touch him as more tears slid down my face.

"What did they do next?"

I pulled my gaze away to watch the men. "They're searching for something. They're mad. One is yelling at the other, asking why they hell he killed him, but the other one isn't answering." I continued describing the chaos I was seeing. "The guy with the gun picked up Faraday's phone as the other one was peering down into an air vent yelling... *I can't fucking get it*. Then the gun guy grabbed the other by the shirt and yanked him off the floor. *Leave it. The cops will never find it.*"

The garage door burst open. "Another guy from the garage walked in and said... It's done."

My eyes flew open. Mason was standing over me and held out his hand to help me stand.

"I'm sorry I couldn't give you more." A tear slid down my cheek. Mason rested his hand on my face and swept the trail of moisture with the pad of his thumb. "You did great."

My eyes slid closed as my heart clenched. I'd done nothing. I couldn't give him a face or even much of a description of the thugs that had done this to Faraday.

"They left something behind," I said, replaying the scene in my mind. I turned in place, scanning the area where the other guy was on the floor. "There." I pointed to the vent near the fireplace. "They left something in there."

Mason dropped his hold and moved quickly to the air vent. He used his keys to work the screws out of place and moved the vent aside before grabbing a pen from the table and pulling the single spent shell casing out of the small area. A smile split his lip as he pulled out his phone and dialed a number. "There was a shell casing left behind at Faraday's. Have a lab tech ready to dust for prints and run ballistics. I'll be back in the office within the hour."

I walked into the kitchen and returned with a sandwich bag for the shell casing. It wasn't much of a find, but I hoped it might help.

"Where was the third guy?" I asked, closing my eyes and trying to remember. I turned toward the garage door.

Leave. Leave now. Urgency slid down my spine as goosebumps covered me from head to toe. *Truth.* Goosebumps were always my sign for when I was interpreting the message dead accurate. A look of sheer panic must have crossed my face.

"What's wrong?"

"We need to go," I answered. "Now. We need to get out."

Mason's brows dipped as he held my gaze. "You're safe here, Blue."

I shook my head. "We need to leave."

I didn't wait around for him to believe me; if I had, I might be waiting for the next ice age. I grabbed my cane and hurried to the door. I adjusted my wig out of my eyes and yanked the door open, trying my best to act like an old woman with a quick gait toward the SUV. I jumped inside, waiting impatiently for Mason to do the same.

Mason was a little slower to follow. He held my gaze as he headed for the SUV. He'd almost made it to the car when the house exploded behind him, sending him crashing against the windshield. A ball of flames exploded into the night sky, and I hurried out of the car and climbed on the hood, resting my fingers on his neck. I closed my eyes, thankful to feel the beat. A sigh of relief left my lips to find that it was strong.

"Run." His eyes shot open, and he held my gaze before his eyes rolled back in his head and his eyes closed once again.

I couldn't run. I couldn't leave him. I grabbed my phone and dialed 911 screaming, "Officer down!" and giving them the address.

The fire was climbing as other little explosions sounded from the house. I grabbed

Mason's keys, and with him still on the hood, I jumped in behind the wheel and moved the SUV farther out of harm's way before climbing back out. I lifted my dress and climbed back up on the hood where Mason was lying unconscious. I was afraid to move him, afraid I might hurt him more.

Move. My gaze scanned the tree line, and I saw a silver glint. *Boom.* I heard the gunshot seconds before feathers were flying around my head. I glanced down at my pillow-encased body. A hole pierced the right side of the dress, with another one on the left. "Crap."

I grabbed Mason by the lapels and rolled with him until we both landed with a grunt on the ground. My breath forcefully whooshed from my lungs, and I struggled to breathe with the weight of Mason's body lying on top of mine. I coughed while struggling to roll him off. I heard the wails of sirens getting closer. Red and blue lights danced through the woods seconds before police and fire vehicles pulled into the driveway and chaos ensued.

One of the detectives came for us, followed by medics. I pointed toward where I'd seen the glint of silver. "There was a shooter in the treeline."

The detective rose from his spot and started barking orders to the others who'd arrived on scene. Several went running for the trees as the firefighters began to unwind their hose.

A medic was working on Mason.

"Are you hurt?"

I yanked out the pillow that I'd wrapped around me underneath the dress. I slid my fingers into one of the holes. "I had a cushion take the shot and break my fall."

His brows dipped, but he ignored the questions I knew he wanted to ask. The wig slipped to the side, and I yanked it off just as Mason's eyes opened for the first time. A groan slipped his lips as he turned away from the paramedic to find me sitting beside him. "You okay?"

I nodded. "You sure know how to show a girl a good time."

His gaze turned to the fire raging in the sky. "You saved us."

"I followed instructions." I grinned. "Something you should try, maybe a bit quicker next time."

The medic helped Mason into a sitting position. "Let's get you in the ambulance. You've got a concussion, and we need to bandage the cuts on your face."

"Which officer showed up first?" he asked the medic and then turned his gaze on me. I shrugged. "I told them there was a shooter in the trees, and they took off running in that direction."

Mason's jaw ticked, and he pushed himself to stand, wobbling on his legs.

"Detective Spencer, you shouldn't be...."

Mason ignored him and rose, holding out his hand to me. "Let's go."

I took his hand, and he paused, staring at the crimson on my hands. "You're hurt?"

I shook my head. "It's not my blood. It's yours."

Mason ran his hand through his hair, and his fingers came away with blood. "Last thing I remember was being on the hood. How did I get to the ground?"

"I moved us both when the first bullet rang out."

"We were shot at? Did you get hit?" he echoed the same question he'd already asked. I seriously considered telling him 'yes,' since that was the answer he was looking for.

I held up the pillow and showed him both holes. "My pillow isn't as fluffy if that's the answer you're looking for."

Mason's legs wobbled, and I quickly wrapped my arm around his waist. "Let's get you to the ambulance."

"I'm all right," he said with slurred words.

"Good, you're a cop and a doctor because I have this pain in my ass. I call him Leonard. Maybe you can prescribe some ointment." Men.

I helped him to the waiting ambulance and watched the medics climb inside to get him lying down on the gurney. They grabbed the doors to shut them, and he stopped them. "She comes with me."

"I'm not hurt," I reiterated like a broken record. I was beginning to think he'd lost some of his brain cells when he bumped his head.

"Someone blew up Faraday's house and then shot at us from the woods. You. Are. Coming. With. Me."

"Really, it's okay. I'll call a friend to pick me up."

He held my gaze, his unrelenting. "They're going to want to question you about why we were here."

"Right," I said, climbing up into the ambulance. "I'm going with him."

"I knew you were smart the first day we met, he said, leaning back onto the gurney.

"You thought I was a nut case." I grinned.

"That too." His eyes slid closed, and he reached for my hand, giving it a gentle squeeze. "Blue, you did good."

"I had a little help."

Chapter 5

I looked ridiculous as I paced outside the ER where mothers cradled their feverish children in their arms and sneezing was becoming an art form. It was just a matter of time before the cops showed up demanding answers that would have me wrapped in a white coat that fastened in the back. I pulled out my phone, my fingers firing across the keyboard as I texted Charlotte.

I need you to come get me. Security at the hospital is eyeing me like I escaped the psych ward.

Hospital? Are you with the badge? Are you okay?

I plopped down in the chair, my fingers hovering over the keyboard as I tried to figure out the words I wanted to use. *The badge is getting X-rays, and Faraday is now homeless.*

Oh, my God.

I need a change of clothes too. Grammy's dress has two bullet holes.

OH. MY. GOD.

I dialed her number, and she picked up on the first ring. "Tell me everything."

"Listen," I said, glancing around the area, "I'll explain everything later, but right now... I need you to come pick me up before the investigating cops show up."

"Do I need to bring your passport?" I glanced at my phone, momentarily shocked.

"Ms. Blue." The nurse behind the desk called my name, and I swung to face her.

"Detective Spencer is requesting you."

"Text me when you're outside the ER," I whispered and ended the call, heading to the door where the nurse was pointing. I stepped inside and didn't miss the way the nurse's snooty gaze traveled over my dress.

"It's laundry day." I shrugged.

Mason was sitting on the bed. The cuts on his face had tiny bandages over them. He wasn't wearing the cheesy hospital gowns that flashed everyone's rear. Shame. I bet his buns were tight just like the rest of his body. Mason's shirtless chest was wrapped up tight. He looked like Humpty Dumpty being put back together again, only this Humpty no one would screw with. He was built with muscles and tattoos as fierce as the scowl on his face.

"You look mad. Did they probe you in the wrong place?" I asked, sitting down on the bed next to him. "Did you like it?"

Mason chuckled. "You're weird."

It was true. "I get told that a lot. I'm glad you're okay."

"I'm glad you are too. Faraday is already going to kill me for taking you there."

I sighed. He was right. Faraday was like my father. He'd stepped right into the role when mine had died. "What's the prognosis?"

"Your people haven't told you yet?"

I peeked behind the veil and spoke the words as they flashed in my mind. "Fractured rib, concussion, and cuts." I nudged his arm. "It's a trifecta. Is this a typical day at the office because, you know, I debated a career choice of becoming a cop and then decided against it because of the stupid itchy uniforms. I'm beginning to believe I made a wise decision."

He pulled out the sandwich baggie from his pocket. "Today was better than a typical day at the office. With this little baby, we're one step closer to finding the thugs that attacked Faraday."

"Are they releasing you? Can you blow this joint? No pun intended." I nudged his arm as I slid off the bed.

"I would hope not," Detective Johnson said from the doorway before he sauntered in.

Johnson looked like a cop. Some people just give off the cop vibe, and he was one of them.

"I guess that's my cue to leave," I said, stepping around him.

His palm caught my arm and moved me back into the room.

I stared at the fingers interrupting the blood circulation in my arm. Two seconds and he'd be leaving here in a finger cast. Huh. I met his gaze. "Do you think they'll put a cast on broken fingers? If I break your middle one then you'll have an excuse for flipping everyone the bird. You can thank me later."

"Johnson." Mason's voice contained enough demand that Johnson released me.

"You aren't going anywhere, Ms. Blue. You can answer my questions here or at the station. The choice is yours."

I met Mason's gaze and read the pity on his face.

"I took her to Faraday's because I believed she could help nail Faraday's assailants."

"Faraday is my case." Johnson glanced between both of us, and then his gaze settled on me. "How did you think you could help? Are you and Faraday friends? Were you a witness? What?"

I pressed my lips together. It would take more than pliers to get me to open. Okay, so I exaggerate. Pliers would ruin my lipstick. Johnson dangling cuffs in front of my face would have me singing like a canary. Still, no metal, no words. I glared daggers at Johnson. He wasn't a bad guy, but he wasn't the head of my cheering team. Maybe I should buy him pompoms. The thought made me grin.

"Just tell him already." Mason's voice was full of resignation. "He's not going to drag you into this. It will make the department look bad."

Ouch. I gawked at Mason and held my hand over my heart in a theatrical show that I did not approve. My time in the high school drama program hadn't been entirely wasted. My tips were beyond reproach. I'd helped provide countless clues for numerous cold cases, even if my efforts went undocumented.

"Faraday is my godfather, and he and my father were best friends. I thought I could help."

"Blue." Mason sighed as he said my name.

"Fine." I tossed my hands up in the air. "I'm psychic. I see dead people, and I know things, but in all fairness, the godfather part is true too. Are you happy now?"

Johnson's mouth parted. That was the standard expression I received when I peeked out of my closet. One day the world would end, and I'd find men and women with pitchforks ready to roast me like a pig over an open pit. It could happen.

I waited as silence filled the room under the scrutiny of his glare.

And waited.

"Believe me, don't believe me, I don't care." My words might have come out a little snappy. I was tired, I was cranky, and the cookie I had for dinner was wearing off. Trying to manipulate and move 230 pounds of pure muscle from the top of an SUV had zapped my cookie calories with the first tug.

Johnson snapped his mouth closed and folded his arms over his chest. "No one is dead in this case."

I pointed my finger at him. "See, that's the thing. I can tap into energy also, and when I do, I can get pictures or words or whatever. It just pops in my mind. I'm clairvoyant. I've got mad skills." I cupped my mouth with one hand and lowered my voice. "But keep that to yourself, yeah? I'm still hiding in my closet pretending to be normal."

Johnson tilted his head, his brows pulled together.

"It was her tip that helped find Sammy Render."

"She could have been in the park that day. She could have seen what was going on and just waited to come forward. Hell, she could have been in on it."

I let out a tired sigh and gave Mason the I-told-you-so annoyed face I reserved for skeptics and the grocer when he runs out of my favorite secret cookie ingredient. I slowly turned back to Johnson and rested my hand on his arm, getting a feel for his energy. I lifted the veil to peek behind the curtain about Johnson and was bombarded with words and pictures in my head. My guides, whom I often called my tribe, were really on their game today.

"Your wife was fired; she was being harassed by her asshole boss. You should really consider suing him for sexual harassment. You'll find she wasn't the only one he was targeting. Your daughter just made all A's and gets picked on because she's quiet. You should buy her a puppy." I grinned and continued. "You just installed new hardwood floors in your house. No, not your house." I gave him a conspiratorial wink. "Your man cave." I pointed to his knee. "Your left knee is throbbing and giving you fits lately. Your cortisone shot is wearing off. You should go see about that while you're here and save yourself a trip."

His gaze remained unfixed, if not hardening a little more. I had that effect on people. Some skeptics didn't like me all up in their business, but Detective Douche was practically begging for proof. My phone vibrated in my hand, and I glanced at the caller ID.

"You can fill him in on everything I picked up on at the house, right?" I turned to leave. Amateur detective hour was over, and I was starting to come up with other ways I might help solve this case.

"Where are you going?" Mason called out.

"My ride is waiting." I spun around at the last minute and snapped my fingers, pointing at Johnson. "There's one part he can't tell you because he was unconscious and out of commission. Someone in the woods shot at us after the house blew. I pulled him off the hood of the SUV to safety, and then you guys showed up." I lifted my Grammy's dress to show him the in-and-out holes from the bullet. "I think that about covers it. Oh, and could you give a message to Faraday for me? Just tell him I'll have his room ready at the house when he breaks out of this place."

They looked at me like I had horns sticking out of my head. I slyly smoothed my hair down before wiggling my fingers as I left. "Later, fellas."

Mason

Chapter 6

Mason couldn't believe he was standing on her doorstep. He'd been standing out there for minutes debating whether he should knock or send a patrol car by to keep an eye on her tonight.

He'd stopped in to break the news to Faraday about his house, and what he and Cree had found, and Faraday had been close to coming unhinged. He'd been annoyed with the news about being homeless but ballistic that Mason had put Cree in harm's way. Mason couldn't blame him. If Cree was Mason's sister, he would have been ready to fight too.

Only Cree and his sister had a ton in common; they both would have gone without permission anyway. Explaining that had been his only saving grace.

Mason had raised his fist to knock when the door swung open.

"Do you need a sleeping bag, or would you like to come in?"

Cree had the apron tied around her body again, and a speck of flour dotted her cheek.

"How did you know I was here? Did you get a flash in your head?"

She grinned like she had all the secrets in the world. "We have security cameras. My dad insisted on it, so I knew the moment you turned in the drive. I would have come out here sooner, but I was afraid dinner would burn."

She left the door open and turned to walk away, leaving him to follow behind her.

"I hope you're hungry. I came home famished, and I've cooked enough for an army."

"You enjoy cooking?"

"Not really, but it helps to drown out the voices in my head." She glanced over her shoulder and grinned.

The smell of oregano and garlic filled the hallway and strengthened as he followed behind her into an industrial-sized kitchen.

Three wedding cakes were sitting on shelves behind a glass door in a huge walk-in fridge.

"So you're a baker?"

"Sort of," she answered. "I'm more like a chemist. I mix and create flavors, enhancing them and turn them into fabulous desserts. The cookie you had earlier was one of my new ones. I called it the Chocolate Buzz cookie."

A pan of lasagna with cheese still bubbling on top was sitting on the counter next to bread sticks and a salad. He peered through the door in the kitchen and into the dining room. Two place settings had been set out in the formal dining room. A small candle between them was unlit.

"Are you expecting company?"

"Just you," she answered, using mittens to carry the lasagna into the dining room. Mason grabbed the breadsticks and salad while she was slipping out of her apron.

"How did you know I'd come by?"

"Because it's something that Faraday would have done. You guys are protectors. It's encoded in your DNA. I just figured I'd feed you while you were here. I hate to eat alone."

"So you guessed."

She grinned but didn't answer as she started to dish portions onto each plate.

"It must be boring to have all the answers ahead of time."

"I don't make a living peering beneath the veils for answers. I don't do it just to aggravate people, no matter what you think. I only use my abilities when and if I can help people."

"And Johnson?"

She chuckled, and her eyes sparkled as she poured wine. "Simple. I needed him off balance so I could leave. He's kind of a douche."

"But he's a good cop. Is it all cops you don't like or just him?"

She gestured to the chair at the end of the table and pulled her plate to the chair next to his so they wouldn't have to holler across the room. "I'm sure he's not a bad guy, just stressed, and who can blame him with what's going on with his family?"

"I'm starting to understand why Faraday was keeping you a secret."

Cree Blue wasn't what she appeared to be. Psychic, sure; baker, absolutely. She could even pass for the southern belle of the Lady Blue Plantation, but something was telling him that Cree had many more secrets she kept hidden beneath the surface. Mason was only seeing what she allowed him to see.

She smiled and slid a bite of lasagna into her mouth, and he did the same.

"So how many cases?" he asked while studying her face. She was beautiful in the girl-next-door kind of way. Her eyes sparkled with mischief as though she'd lived each day like it might be her last.

"I'll make you a deal. For each question you ask, you have to answer one of mine."

"Last time we made a deal, you almost died."

"Uh, wrong again. You almost died." She grinned and took another bite.

"Okay, so how many?"

"How many cold cases have we attempted, or how many actually ended up helping to solve the case?"

"Both."

She tapped her fork against her lip. "Between my father and myself, we've had fifty-four local attempts and thirty-two that resulted in either additional clues or the case getting solved."

Mason broke the bread, popped it into his mouth and started chewing while mulling over her answers. "What do you mean by local? Do you have a string of detectives like Faraday around the country that you help?"

She pointed her fork at him. "You skipped my turn."

He shrugged. She didn't miss a beat.

"Who is Moreno?"

"Dominique Moreno is a local crime boss that was just arrested for murder and is awaiting trial in the county jail."

She slowly nodded her head as if thinking it over.

"Now, what exactly did you mean by local? Do you have more than one detective like Faraday that you're helping?"

"He's the only badge," she answered. "What kind of evidence do you have on Moreno?"

"We had a smoking gun with his fingerprints." He didn't even give her time to process. "Who do you help that isn't local?"

She sat quietly and took another bite of her food as if mulling over her answer, and he knew that was exactly what she was doing.

"It depends. Sometimes I'll be watching the news and I get flashes of the real killer or if someone is innocent. If it's important, then I'll send the other agencies a letter or call in an anonymous tip. It's up to them if they want to follow up on it. I don't hide how I came up with the information. I'm upfront when I tell them that I'm a psychic. I just leave my name out of it."

"So that's why Faraday is big on keeping your identity a secret."

"I guess." She smiled. "Who do you think these three guys were that attacked Faraday?"

"I'd just be guessing if I answered that."

"Okay, so guess." She took another bite of food.

"My gut tells me it was three of Moreno's thugs."

"Has Johnson questioned them?" she asked.

Mason wasn't sure. He would think that Johnson had, but Mason didn't remember seeing any statements in Faraday's file. "The case is fresh. I'm sure they're working hard on solving who did this to Faraday. He's a cop. That means the whole force is gunning to catch the people responsible. You skipped my turn."

"I'll make you a doggie bag of cookies to take home."

Mason chuckled, leaning back in his chair. He could still tell that something was bothering Cree. "You're safe here."

"I know," she said, taking a sip of her wine. "My dad and Grammy made sure of that. The Lady Blue will keep me safe."

With that, their conversation turned into more normal things like hobbies and what they each liked to do for fun. They were as different as night and day. Her hobby was baking; where he ate most of his food from takeout. She liked to garden, and he didn't have a green thumb and couldn't keep a cactus alive. She was in charge of fundraisers, and the thought of even attending one in a monkey suit had him scratching his collar. When the topic of family came up, she'd maneuvered the conversation in an entirely different direction. It was a subtle shift, but one he was trained to catch. The more they talked, the more he started to understand. Cree Blue was a normal person, if not highly motivated, except for the fact that somehow she knew things that no one could explain. Two hours later, she made good on her word and walked him to the door with a doggie bag full of leftovers and cookies in his hands.

"Are you going to be okay here the rest of the night?"

She rested her hand on the door as he stepped out onto the veranda. "Why wouldn't I be?"

"Someone shot at you today. That would make normal people a little scared."

"You said it yourself earlier. I'm not normal, and technically, I think they were shooting at you. I was just an old lady on the scene."

There was something about her response that left him believing that the woman he'd spent the last two hours with wasn't actually the true Cree Blue, just the bits and pieces she'd precisely picked for him to see.

"Good night, Leonard."

He chuckled and stepped down the stairs. "Good night, Blue."

Chapter 7

I jogged up the stairs to find Grammy's and my mother's apparitions standing at the window. Both of them looked as though if they had scorecards they would each be holding up a number.

"He's going to see you," I growled and moved to flick the curtains closed.

"He's a solid ten, honey," Grammy announced, dispersing and reappearing on the other side of the room.

"Make him work for it," Mom announced before disappearing out of the room.

"Don't listen to her, honey. Life is too short not to enjoy every moment. Be glad your daddy ain't here. He would have rattled chains to run the pretty cop away. No man will ever be good enough for his little girl," Grammy said, gliding out of the room.

Where was my father, and why hadn't he dropped in like mom and Gram? I mulled that thought over. It didn't make sense that he hadn't appeared. Was he avoiding me on purpose?

The Lady Blue Plantation had about twenty ghosts that liked to visit. People from Grammy's past and ancestors who'd died long before I was born. They were like an extension of me in a sense. Each had their own reason for showing up and hanging out, and yet, I couldn't help but feel there was a ton they'd never share with me.

I tossed and turned all night. My mind was working overtime to come up with a way to help Faraday with more than just putting a roof over his head. Someone was dead, Faraday had almost joined them, and a mob boss was sitting in jail awaiting trial. There was only one person who had the answers I needed, and lucky for me, it wasn't like he was going anywhere anytime soon. A plan started to form, and a smile split my lips.

"I wonder if he likes cookies."

****

I started out bright and early making calls to the prison to figure out how to do this whole visit-a-convict thing, and thank God I did. They had a crap-ton of rules, and just scanning their list I would have broken twenty, and that was just getting through security. I loaded the cookies anyway, knowing full well and good that they wouldn't even reach Moreno. I wasn't bringing him my chocolaty deliciousness; I was taking them to the guards instead. I wouldn't consider it bribery, maybe more like southern hospitality for their taste buds. A southern girl was taught never to show up without the proper gifts.

I signed in on the log and passed my ID to the person running checks to make sure I didn't have any warrants or that I belonged in jail. Her gaze landed on my tin, and her brow rose.

"Officer"—I glanced at the name tag— "Deputy Shaw." I smiled. "I wasn't bringing my cookies for the inmate; I brought them for you guys. I opened the lid and slightly lifted them so they could see I hadn't planted a bomb and there were no hidden shanks baked into my recipe. I took one out and bit into it so she could see that I hadn't poisoned them either.

Capping the container, I slid it through the opening and went to take my seat. Ten minutes later Deputy Shaw called me back up to the window. A smudge of chocolate sat at the corner of her lip. The deputies behind her each had a cookie in their hands. She smiled and slid my license back, along with a locker key. "All personal items must be placed in the locker before you go through the metal detector."

"Thanks."

I'd turned to walk off when my inner radar started to tingle ever so slightly. I turned back to Shaw. "Excuse me for asking, but have you recently lost your grandmother?"

She lifted a brow but didn't answer either way. I didn't need her to. I was already getting the message loud and clear.

I smiled sweetly and met her gaze. "She wants you to know her will is inside her favorite book and she left you her house. She says you'll need the big kitchen because she expects you to carry on the family traditions and she expects you personally to take over making the pecan pies at Thanksgiving. She says you're the better cook out of all the grandkids."

Officer Shaw's gaze softened, even if her lips remained unmoving.

"She's kind of a no-nonsense lady." I grinned. "Sort of reminds me of you."

Still no answer of acknowledgment. "Okay then." I tapped the counter before spinning around and retaking my seat.

Thirty minutes later I was sitting at a round table in the visiting area. Relatives, loved ones, and a few shady characters were all waiting anxiously nearby. When the door buzzed, all the men in prison grays entered. Their faces lit up as the cons dispersed like a drop of oil in a bucket of water.

One man remained, letting his gaze wander around the room, and instantly I knew he was Moreno. I waved at him and slowly rose from my seat as he neared.

"Who are you?" he asked, gazing at me skeptically.

"Cree Blue," I answered and gestured to the seat across the table. "Please have a seat, Mr. Moreno."

He sat down, I think more out of curiosity than anything else. "What do you want?"

"I want the names of the people you sent after Detective Faraday."

His brows dipped, and he tilted his head. "Open your eyes, lady. I'm in prison, and not a single one of my family members are here to see me. How do you expect me to place a hit on anyone from inside here, not that I'm the type of man who would place a hit."

"Of course you're not." I rolled my eyes and, folding my arms, rested them on the table. "Mr. Moreno, Faraday is my godfather, and he's currently in the hospital. I understand you don't know me, so let me tell you who I am, and then I'm going to ask you that question again."

"You don't scare me, lady," he growled.

"I'm a psychic and a medium. I help the police solve cold cases, and if you don't tell me what I want to know, I'll make it my life mission to work on only cases that you're a suspect in."

He smirked.

Wrong answer.

Visions came quick and fast. "I'll start with tuning in on your accounting and creative books." I chewed my lips. "You don't keep the real ones in a typical wall safe. You have your own vault. Thirty-four, seventeen..." I raised a brow. "Should I continue?"

He didn't answer one way or the other if I was right. I wasn't really expecting him to jump up and say "Oh my God, you're for real." That would have been too easy.

"If you're the real deal, then you know that I didn't commit the crime they pinned on me."

His words caught me off guard, so I peeked beyond the veil. Visions flooded my mind, first of him and a blonde woman in a Jacuzzi getting intimate and then of someone with a shorter frame than he had squeezing the trigger.

"You're right. You might be responsible for many things, but you didn't pull that trigger. Why were your fingerprints found on the gun?"

"That's simple. I'm being framed for killing the librarian. Do I even look like the type of guy that hangs out in a library? I'm telling you I never crossed paths with the missing woman."

"Don't you mean dead woman?"

"They haven't produced a body, only matching DNA from blood that was found at the crime. When they do find the librarian's body, they'll have no choice but to arrest the right guy, which isn't me."

Goosebumps. Truth. Call it intuition, call it the tingle in my gut, but I knew he was telling me the truth.

"Are we done here?" he asked, rising.

"No." I was quick to answer. "I'll make you deal. You call off your thugs and get me a name on Faraday's shooter, and I'll find the librarian's body."

He sat back down. "Listen, lady, I told you I had nothing to do with whatever you're accusing me of."

My eyes narrowed. "You have a long reach, Moreno. Call off your goons and use your influence to help me find out who shot my godfather, and I'll help you by solving the mystery around the librarian's death."

"And if I say no?" he asked, crossing his arms over his chest, his beady eyes narrowed to daggers.

"Then expect a slew of charges and evidence from other crimes to magically appear."

"How do I know you won't do it anyway?"

"You don't, but I promise that I won't go *actively* searching for the crimes you've already committed. Now, if a cold case were to cross my desk, and you happen to be implicated in a crime, then that's another story. But trust me when I tell you, you don't want me to put the full force of my focus on you. I'm a true southern lady, and we never give up."

I rose from my seat and rested my hands on the table. "And if you even think about sending someone to shut me up, you better be certain you know all my secrets because the location of your *real* books will be sent to the FBI before they bury my body. I can promise you that."

"You've got moxy, lady. No one under my command would even think of threatening me."

"There's not much I wouldn't do for the people I love."

"You've got a deal," he said, rising to stand. "I'll see what I can do on your case, and you investigate mine. I'll call you if I find out anything."

"You don't have my number."

His lips twisted into a grin. "You're Grammy Blue's granddaughter and Phillip Blue's kid. You live at the Lady Blue Plantation, and I've tasted your cookies. I know how to reach you, and I'm not even psychic."

Chapter 8

I was escorted back out to the waiting area where the lockers were pressed against the wall. Deputy Shaw was leaning against the lockers, her arms folded over her chest.

"My mother found the will right where you said it would be."

"That's great." Not that I doubted they wouldn't.

"You helped me, so let me give you a little piece of advice."

"Oh?" I asked, sliding my key into the locker and twisting to retrieve my car keys and wallet.

"I don't know why you're here to visit Moreno, but he isn't the kind of man you want to get mixed up with. He's dangerous and cunning, and he'll use you to get what he wants."

I rested my hand on her arm. "I appreciate your concern and thanks for the heads-up, but I'm the one using him for the information I need."

I walked out of the building to find Detective Mason Spencer leaning against my car.

"What are you doing here?" I asked as I approached.

"I could ask you the same thing."

"I came to see Moreno."

His jaw ticked, and he ran his hand over his head. I hit the fob and opened my car door, letting him process what I'd said.

To his credit, it looked like he was barely containing his anger when he said one simple word. "Why?"

I let out a long sigh. "The guy in my vision said his name and then you—"

"Don't blame this on me," he growled.

"Well, you did *guess* that it was him. You should take that as a compliment that I believed you."

"You're going to end up as dead as the librarian he's accused of killing."

"He's innocent of that crime." I cringed even saying the words, but they were true. "Besides, why would he kill me if I'm the only person who can help him prove he's innocent?"

I went to shut the door, but Mason held it open. "You aren't a cop or a private investigator."

"Thanks for the reminder, again," I said as another plan filled my mind. "But I have a knack of seeing things that others don't." I grinned and left him speechless in the parking lot.

I had things to do, things that would have the cops super pissed at me when they found out I was trying to help a known crime boss beat the charges that were filed against him. It was possible that when I was done they'd never let me help on another cold case again.

I arrived at the Lady Blue Plantation to find Jitters and Charlotte sitting on the porch drinking iced tea. They looked as though they didn't have a care in the world. I jogged up the steps to the veranda and joined them sitting in my Grammy's favorite rocking chair.

"Where are the others?"

"Doc is in surgery, and Winston is still dealing with family stuff. The twins are out of town, but we're here for you," Charlotte announced, handing me a sweet tea that she had waiting.

I took a long sip and momentarily closed my eyes to absorb energy from the Lady Blue. This old plantation had a way of calming me.

My eyes slid open to find both Jitters and Charlotte staring at me.

"I need your help," I said, rising and heading inside. "I need whatever you can find on the disappearance of the town librarian."

"I'm on it," Jitters announced, sliding in behind his favorite computer. Within seconds, the screens illuminated as Charlotte took her seat.

"What are we looking for?"

I paced the open area of the ballroom where the hospital bed normally sat when we worked on cold cases. I liked to keep all of that stuff stored away in a special secure space when it wasn't in use.

"Name for starters, the evidence that was reported, a picture of her, her address, anything and everything we can find. I need to find a connection that I can tap into."

"Can I ask why?" Charlotte asked as images of online newspaper articles started to appear on screens.

"I made a deal with the devil." Butterflies took flight in my belly as the hairs on my arms stood up. I'd actually made a freakin' deal with the devil. Realization settled in my gut, and I let out a shaky breath. "Find what happened to the librarian, and I get the name of Faraday's shooter."

An image of Moreno filled a part of the screen; it was the photo of him in handcuffs.

Charlotte slowly rose from her seat and pointed to the screen. "Tell me that you did not talk to that man."

I cringed. "I did more than talk. I threatened him."

Charlotte rested her fist on her waist and lowered her head, shaking it in disapproval, kind of like that time I was five and stood on the roof, wearing a cape and ready to fly like the birds.

"Margarete Stead was reported missing a month ago. Sources say there was no sign of forced entry and nothing was missing from the house."

"Then why do they suspect foul play?" Charlotte asked, turning toward the screen.

"A gun," I announced.

"Ding, ding, ding. They found a gun on site that was connected to Moreno. They found bullet holes in a pillow and blood splatter on the sheets." Jitter's announced.

"And?" I asked, folding my arms over my chest.

"That's it," he said, pulling up several more photos of the crime scene and a picture of a pretty brunette at the library.

"How did they determine the blood belonged to the librarian?"

A few more clicks and we were looking at the coroner's report. "Looks like they tested the DNA against the hair in her brush."

"We may have a dead librarian, but Moreno didn't do this, even if he is a bad seed."

"How do you know?"

I gave Charlotte a look of duh.

"Well, if you saw the incident, then who killed her and where is the body?"

"That's what I need to figure out," I answered. "I need something personal of hers."

A few clicks later and a rental sign popped up on the screen. "How about visiting the crime scene and putting out your energy feelers or whatever it is that you do?"

"You're a genius," I announced. My voice may have squealed as I pulled out my cell phone and dialed the number on the rental sign. Within the next ten minutes, I set up a meeting with the realtor about rental properties. She'd sounded surprised, if a little hesitant, when I gave her the property address. I'd been speechless when she told me that the house was no longer available. She'd then proceeded to give me the list of other houses in the same neighborhood that were similar in size and structure. I reluctantly agreed and set up a time and place to meet her.

"Pull up the surrounding rental properties and tell me which one is closest to that house."

A list of houses filled the screen; one of the properties was right next door, the others around the block. My choice was easy.

The next two hours had me riding around the neighborhood with the realtor looking at rental places I didn't need, in a subdivision where everything looked cloned and nothing was original. The houses were all the same; one-story modest ranch houses with the bushes and landscape impeccable. Kids played in the yards and a few in the streets. There was nothing remarkable that stood out, no lingering shadows, nothing even with bling that would draw lowlifes into this area. These were blue-collar people, so unless a thief had inside knowledge of treasures the librarian was hiding behind her walls, then there was no reason to believe these people had much to steal.

Taking that into account, and the fact there had been no forced entry, the culprit had to be someone in her inner circle. Someone she would have welcomed into her home and potentially into her bed since that was where the crime occurred. If that were the case, they wouldn't have arrested Moreno seeing as how he'd been getting busy with a blonde that night.

I knew the place instantly when we pulled up. The vibes coming from the home next door were like a living, breathing energy that oozed from the bricks. I got out of the car and immediately started across the lawn.

"Ms. Blue, the house for rent is over here," the lady called out.

I stopped and stared at the home. If I could just steal a couple minutes inside…

"Ms. Blue," she called out again.

"Who lives here?" I asked, already knowing the answer.

"No one currently," the lady announced, walking to my side. She must have realized that I wasn't moving until she answered. "That property isn't on the market yet. The librarian lived there."

"Oh?" I asked. "Did she move?"

"She went missing. The cops suspect foul play but can't find the body."

"I'll take it," I announced.

"Oh, that one's not the one for rent."

I pointed to the one I hadn't even seen. "I meant that one. I'll take it."

"But wouldn't you like to see the inside first?"

I turned away from the house I wanted to peek inside and back to the woman. I smiled sweetly and gestured to the house next door. "Of course, show me the way."

The house she showed me was tiny compared to the Lady Blue, but it was clean and had all the required amenities. The white picket fence went all the way around the house, encompassing the pool in the backyard. Beyond that was a playground and pavilion. "What is that used for?"

"Community parties and cookouts. This is a very tight-knit community that embraces its members."

"Sounds perfect." I hope my voice didn't give away my reservations. I was starting to feel like maybe I'd walked straight into the pages of the *Stepford Wives* or into the layer were all serial killers live unnoticed. Unlike the librarian, I'd be sleeping with one eye open.

"Excellent." The realtor beamed. "We just need you to fill out some paperwork, and once your check clears, then you can move in when you're ready."

I planned on it, just like I planned to sneak into the librarian's house to see if I could pick up any vibes to get to the answers I needed.

Chapter 9

Charlotte and I smiled like all southern women do when they're expected to be nice but also smart enough to be leery of others' motives. The pavilion across the field got closer with every step. Apparently, they'd planned a come-out-and-meet-the-neighbors party, and I was the guest of honor. Personally, I knew they were deciding if I was Stepford-wife material.

"Tell me again why it's a good deal to make friends with these people."

I wrapped my arm around hers and grinned. "People love to gossip. We just have to prod them with the right subject."

"So around a mouthful of hors d'oeuvres you're just going to ask, who killed the librarian?"

"Of course not," I teased. "I'm going to find out who had motive and make my own conclusions."

Charlotte rolled her eyes. "They better be serving alcoholic beverages with little umbrellas."

I glanced her way, and my face turned serious. "Don't drink their Kool-Aid. Stick with sealed bottles that you open yourself," I leaned in to whisper. "Anyone or all of these people could be killers."

Charlotte spun around like she was about to go back to the rental when I steered her back around in the direction of the pavilion. "You're the eyes in the back of my head."

"And who is watching my back?"

"There you are," Ms. Stallman announced. She'd been the first to arrive at my door the day we'd been unloading a few essentials to look like I was actually going to live there. The brownies she'd given me were made with a special blend reserved for college campuses. If the one-woman welcoming committee had been wanting to get me stoned, there was no telling what might happen at this party.

Ms. Stallman stood on one of the picnic table seats and clapped her hands together to get everyone's attention. "Everyone, this is Cree Blue... and her friend." Henrietta Stallman looked down her nose at Charlotte, who stood out like a turkey running the fields on Thanksgiving. Most everyone was dressed casually, except I was in a little sundress and Charlotte was wearing ripped jeans and a T-shirt that did little to complement her figure. The men looked us over as if debating if we'd be dessert, and a few of the women raised their brows.

"Let's all be hospitable and welcome them into the Shady Oaks community."

"Let's not," Charlotte whispered, and it took the full strength of my resolve not to grin.

The women from the group slowly surrounded us like wild cats and we were their prey, looking for the perfect place to strike our jugulars.

The tall blonde leader of the group stopped in front of me. Her gaze lingered, down to my shoes and back up. "I'm Ava. I live in the house across the street from yours."

"Nice to meet you, Ava." I held out my hand, but Ava didn't shake it. She was the suspicious type. I could read it in her eyes and her ugly aura.

Ava crossed her arms over her chest and lifted her wine glass to her lips, taking a sip. "Are you two a couple?"

I exchanged a look with Charlotte and debated how I wanted to answer that question. Of course, Charlotte and I were just best friends, but these people didn't know that.

"There you are, honey." Mason's voice came from behind before his arms wrapped around my waist. His breath was hot against my skin before he pressed his lips to my cheek. "Sorry, I'm late. I lost track of time."

Ava's shoulders immediately relaxed. "Perfect, you're married. We were worried about having another single woman living on this street."

"Oh, we aren't married." I smiled up at Mason.

"Yet. I've asked, and I'm just waiting for her to say yes. Isn't that right, sugar?" Mason's voice was full of warning. His warm fingers rested on my stomach.

I raised my brow and turned back to the women. "Something like that."

"Excuse me," Charlotte interjected. "What happened the last time a single woman lived on this street?"

"The librarian," a tiny brunette standing next to Ava announced.

"Marcie," Ava growled in warning, the way a southern woman was trying to be sugar sweet but reminding the group she still had claws.

"She needs to know," Marcie continued. "The librarian lived in the house next door. She vanished in the middle of the night."

"It had to be that boyfriend of hers," another lady announced. "He looked like a thug."

I glanced up at Mason; his brows were furrowed. Apparently, the police didn't know about a potential boyfriend. I sure didn't.

"Who was the boyfriend?" Charlotte asked.

"Oh, we don't know his name. She didn't introduce us," Marcie announced.

The other girl picked up where Marcie stopped. "I've only seen him come around at night."

"Ooh. He sounds mysterious," I cooed. "Was he good looking? Did he seem rich? Were they an item for long?"

"It's not polite to gossip, Marcie," Ava announced and spun around and headed to where the men were standing.

"Sorry." Marcie frowned. "We aren't supposed to talk about it."

I gave Marcie an understanding smile. "Why is that?"

"The whole incident has left a dark cloud over the neighborhood."

Mason's arms tightened around my waist.

"I thought I saw signs of a neighborhood watch," Charlotte said, resting her hands on her hips.

"A few houses have cameras, but we don't technically have a neighborhood watch. I mean we look out after each other and report suspicious activity…"

"Who do you report it to?" Mason asked.

"Ava and her husband, Hank," Marcie answered.

"Marcie," Ava called out, and we turned to find Ava and her husband staring at us.

"Sorry. I've got to go. It was nice meeting you all. I live next door to you, Cree. Feel free to stop by if you need anything."

"Thanks and the same goes for you," I said while slipping out of Mason's arms.

We all watched her walk off, and then I turned my glare on Mason and crossed my arms over my chest. "How did you know where to find me?"

"You're sticking your nose where it doesn't belong," he answered. "This is an active investigation, and any one of those people could be the killer."

"Actually, I was leaning more toward the mysterious boyfriend," Charlotte interrupted.

"Detective Spencer, you didn't answer my question. How did you find me?"

His eyes searched mine, and the more I thought about it, the more I was beginning to understand. "Come to think about it, how did you know I went to the jail?"

"He must have a tracker on your car," Charlotte answered and covered her mouth when he didn't say one way or another if she was correct. "Oh, Detective. I thought you were smarter than that."

I balled my fists at my sides, and my glare turned into daggers. "You need to leave, *sugar*."

He reached for my arm, and I took a step back. "Cree, let me explain."

"Leave. Now."

"I'm not going to apologize for watching your back. God knows someone needs to. You walk right into danger without a second thought about your own safety, and you drag your friends into it with you. Now I'm starting to understand why Faraday didn't let you investigate the active cases." He leaned in to whisper in my ear, "You're going to get yourself killed."

"Goodbye, Detective." My words were a whisper between us, the tone unrelenting as anger stirred through my veins.

"Watch your back, Cree. Even if you figure out who the killer is, you aren't equipped to stop him from coming after you," He said before stomping off and disappearing around the corner of my house.

"He's got a point. You're never this close to the action," Charlotte said, wrapping her arm around mine and turning me back to the neighborhood party.

"If I could get my hands on something personal of Margarete Stead's, then I wouldn't need to be this close." I glanced over my shoulder back to the librarian's house. The house stood empty. The curtains were open, showing no furniture or personal items were inside. I wasn't even sure if I could get a hit off the energy with everything already gone. This sucked.

"You know there's more than one way to find something personal of hers."

My gaze snapped to Charlotte's.

"She had a job. Everyone takes personal items to their jobs, and even most people might talk about their husband or boyfriends to their co-workers. I would lay money that they might have more answers than these people."

"You're brilliant."

"I have my moments."

"I don't know why I didn't think of that."

"Might have saved yourself first and last month's rent and a security deposit, not to mention having to meet all of these weird people. I don't know about you, but they give me the willies." She turned to look at me and let out a tired breath. "Can we leave now?"

"Of course we can. I need to renew my library card."

Chapter 10

I wasn't going to take Charlotte with me to the library. The more I thought about what Mason had said, the more I was realizing that he was right. Not about all things, but about pulling my friends into danger. I sent her to the Lady Blue instead with the idea that she'd watch over things there. She'd been reluctant to go almost to the point of stomping back out to the gathering and announcing she was my lesbian lover.

Logic prevailed when I explained I might need Insight up and running if I actually found something of Margarete's I could use. She'd gone back, but under duress, and was adamant I be careful.

I had a restless night and barely slept. I was a light sleeper anyway, but for every creak and unexplainable nose, I investigated. Once I'd even spotted Ava and her husband out walking on the sidewalk at midnight. My guides and inner voice weren't screaming at me to run. I didn't feel like I was in danger. It was a creepy vibe like the one I'd picked up on at the party. Maybe it was just my overactive imagination thinking one of these people was responsible for committing the heinous crime.

I locked up and left my house with important errands on my mind. As I rode through the neighborhood, I could feel the eyes on me as I passed. The unique feeling that came with being watched. I slowly scanned each house and window, trying to locate the target of my unease, and yet there was nothing. No one out on the streets, no open windows, or even anything peeking from behind the slats. Yet the feeling was undeniable and unshakable.

I turned out of the subdivision and drove the ten minutes into downtown where the library sat at the end of Main Street. I parked and stared up at the old building. The old red bricks were worn and crumbling. The concrete sidewalk up to the door was cracked and in need of replacing. I could only imagine what things looked like on the inside.

A woman and group of younger kids carrying books came out of the door as I was about to enter. Each just chatted away about why their book was better than the ones the siblings had picked.

I walked into the library and paused inside the door. Where the outside had been rundown, and in need of an overhaul, the inside looked like the Taj Mahal. Murals were painted on the high stone cathedral ceiling. There were three floors of railings and books. There was an old lady standing behind the checkout counter scanning books. I slowly walked around. Tables and computers were strategically placed around the room. A central clump of computers sat on a round table where patrons could go look up book locations. Men were on laptops, and women scanned the blurbs on the back of the books. It was typical library, even if the setup was grander than most I'd ever seen.

An electrical energy filled the air, contradicting the quietness in the building. I loved places like this. Where things were never as they seemed.

Portraits of the town's librarians, past and present, lined the walls, surrounding the pictures of the library building when each had worked. I felt like I was stepping back in time the further I moved down the line until I got to the old-timey yellowing picture of when the first building was built on the land.

"Incredible," I whispered, wondering which building my Grammy Blue would have visited when she was a little girl.

"Isn't it?" A woman clutching books to her chest came up beside me to look at the pictures. "The history of this building and the librarians before me are rich with color and stories. Some might even suggest their ghosts linger and have never left."

"You work here?" I asked, glancing her way and realizing her picture wasn't one on the wall.

"Yep, I'm one of the lucky ones. I was hired a month ago. They haven't added my picture to the wall yet. I have to be here for a year before they consider me a permanent employee."

"Oh," I said, moving back down to the current librarians. I pointed to Margarete's picture. "You replaced Margarete?"

The librarian let out a sigh. "It's hard to get a job as a librarian. Each librarian loves their job and normally stays so long in the position they retire from it. Poor Margarete wasn't so lucky. It's sad really. The patrons loved her and still come in asking for her by name. Even though she was only here six months, she still made an impression."

"If she wasn't here a year, why is her picture on the wall?"

"Since the newspapers and police think she's dead and died as a librarian, she was given all the accolades that go with the job," the woman announced as if it all made perfect sense.

This chick was acting as if the women on the walls died while serving our country and gave their lives to do it.

"What if she's not dead?" I asked and glanced at the librarian.

"I don't know." Her brows dipped. "I guess they'd take her picture down and I might lose my job. You don't think that's the case do you?" Her voice rose in tone.

"I doubt they'd fire you without reason. They might just take her picture down." I patted the woman's arm to calm her down. The last thing I needed was to deal with a hysterical librarian who was afraid she might lose her job. "I barely knew Margarete, but I heard nice things about her. I heard she met her boyfriend here," I lied.

"Boyfriend?" the woman echoed. "No, I don't think so. I had to clean out her desk, and there weren't any pictures of a boyfriend. The only picture she had on her desk was of her and Mandy Stuart, her best friend, while on vacation."

"Have you met her best friend?"

"Of course." The woman smiled. "Mandy comes in here all the time to visit her mother, Glenda. She's the head librarian."

"What did you do with the picture?" I asked as I continued walking farther out of ear shot from the old librarian. The last thing I needed was her asking who in the heck I was.

"I think the police have her things," she answered.

"Thanks for your time. I'm just going to go look around and find something to read."

The hair on my nape prickled as I slowly scanned each level of the library. Someone was watching again. I could feel it to my core. Two men were across the room, both wearing dark pants and Hawaiian shirts. Neither of them looked like typical readers. Maybe husbands looking for some way to kill time? Or potential killers reading a how-to book?

One had a magazine in his hand, flipping the pages; the other guy had his gaze locked on me.

I slipped my phone out of my pocket and texted Mason. *Mandy Stuart is the librarian's best friend. Have you questioned her?*

Stop investigating, was the quick reply I received back. His demands made me smile. I think we both knew that his suggestion was just that... a suggestion.

I need something personal of the librarian's, and unless you give me something to work with, I have to find something myself. Besides...I think I'm onto something. I took a picture of the two men watching me and texted him that too.

I didn't wait around for his reply before I shoved the phone back into my pocket and headed straight for the two men, who were now scowling at me. Aw. Poor guys must be camera-shy.

"Cree Blue," I said and held out my hand.

"We know who you are, Ms. Blue."

"Well, if you know who I am, why not level the playing field and tell me who you are?"

The big six-foot-two man with the clean-shaved head grinned. "We're your new bodyguards. I'm Freddie, and this here is George."

Well, I hadn't been expecting that. "Who sent you? Mason? Charlotte? Faraday? Because you can just go back and tell them I don't need protecting."

"Mr. Moreno gave us explicit instructions to watch your back while you work on setting him free."

I rested my hand on my hip. "Yeah, see, here's the thing. I'm not working on getting him free. I'm working to find a potential killer."

My words came out a little louder than I'd expected as aggravation seeped into my voice. A group of college-aged students sitting near us were staring as if expecting the thugs to rob me.

"Either way, you're working on getting him out." The large Italian shrugged. "Just continue doing your thing. You'll never even know we're here."

"Tell your boss I'm still waiting on a name." I spun in place and glanced over my shoulder as I started to leave the building, pointing from my eyes to theirs and back again in the universal sign that I'd be watching them, watching me. They remained ten paces behind me like a solid wall of muscle and I was some movie star that they'd take a bullet for. Their presence was hard to miss, scary and intimidating as hell.

I pulled out my phone again and fired off the best friend's name to Jitters to see what he might be able to find and told him I'd be by soon. Just as I hit Send, I had an incoming text from Mason.

I'll meet you in your new rental, and watch your back, Blue. Those are Moreno's guys.

I grinned and shoved the phone back into my pocket as I hopped inside my Jeep.

I needed something only Mason could currently give me. I could have threatened him with going public about using a psychic, but I was saving that little gem for when I really needed it.

Mason

Chapter 11

Cree's neighborhood was quiet in a way that Mason expected most people lived. Kids played out in the yards. Women wearing spandex jogged up and down the streets with their dogs on leashes. A man wearing a suit pulled into the drive three houses down, stopped, and picked up a bicycle that a kid had left out. This was typical suburbia. The kind of life Mason had tried to live.

Roses were wilting and dying in the garden outside the librarian's house. The house on the other side of Cree's was just the opposite, almost in a nauseating, overpowering way. Everything in that lady's garden was pink and on steroids.

The female neighbor waved, and Mason smiled back. He guessed she took that as an invitation since she was cutting through the yard in his direction.

"She hasn't given you a key yet?"

"Not yet," he answered, kicking the overnight bag he had at his feet, even though it didn't have his clothes in it. It had something much more important to Cree.

"I'm Marcie. I live next door." She glanced at my holster. "I see you're a cop. I'm sure the whole neighborhood will feel safer when you move in."

He just slowly nodded. He had no intention of living in this neighborhood, much less letting Cree stay too much longer. That was why he was here.

Marcie was a cute girl, but nothing like Cree. Where Cree had a timeless girl next door beauty that seemed effortless, Marcie appeared to be trying too hard. Her makeup was too thick, her tank top too tight, and her shorts barley covered her ass. She'd left little to the imagination.

"I was just admiring your garden."

"I'm good with my hands." She winked.

Cree pulled into the drive, wearing a baseball cap, and got out of her Jeep. She smiled before glancing up and down the street.

"There you are."

She walked over to him, and Mason rested his arm over her shoulder and pulled her in tight.

Cree glanced up at him and then back at Marcie, taking the hint. She wrapped her arm around his waist. "Thanks for keeping my honey company."

Marcie's cheeks pinked. "Anytime."

Her words dripped with double meaning.

Marcie walked off, and Cree headed for the door. "My neighbor likes you."

He didn't even respond to that comment as he followed Cree to the door. She'd paused with her key poised for the lock when she took a step back. She pointed to where the door wasn't pulled all the way closed.

"When I left, that was closed and locked."

Mason handed Cree the overnight bag. "Isn't this a little presumptuous?"

Mason just shook his head and pulled his gun from the holster. "Wait here."

She nodded for once, not fighting him.

Mason made quick work out of silently clearing each room, checking for an intruder or any sign that someone had been in the house. Nothing even remotely looked out of place. He returned to the door and held it open for her to enter. "Nothing looks out of place."

She slowly moved around the room, disappearing toward her bedroom before returning. "Maybe I was wrong."

"I don't like you living here," he said moving to the French doors to look outside. "You don't even have any security."

"Actually…" She paused until he turned around. "Moreno sent me Freddie and George."

She was on the first-name basis with Moreno's right-hand muscle. He'd screwed up royally by taking her to Faraday's house and getting her mixed into this mess. This was all on him.

"What have you found out?"

"The librarian was likable. People still come in asking for her. It's possible she had a stalker, or some sicko just followed her home from the library. It could have been anyone. You should check out the library and see if they had surveillance."

"I'm sure the investigators already covered it, but I'll check again when I get back." Mason walked over to her and stopped in front of her. He rested his palm on her cheek. "These are dangerous people, Cree. What's it going to take to get you to walk away?"

"Finding the librarian."

He had a feeling she was going to say that. The truth was written in her eyes. Cree would do pretty much anything for the people she cared about. He slowly nodded. "Good, then let's find the librarian."

Mason grabbed his overnight bag and set it on the table. He unzipped it and pulled out one of the evidence bags like the one she'd given him the first time they met. "They didn't collect much from the crime scene, but I brought you the bloody sheet."

Cree smiled, the kind that reached her eyes, and he was finding he liked it more and more. "You believe me."

Lesser men might have shrugged off her words, but there was nothing lesser about Mason. He understood the impact of that statement and what it might actually mean to her. "I believe you know things you shouldn't possibly know. I believe you have a good heart and protect the people you care about. I believe in you."

Her cheeks turned a pretty shade of pink as she closed the distance between them. She stared up into his eyes. The pools of hers were vibrant and clear. Mason lowered his head, his mouth hovering near hers.

"I have to go out of town, but when I get back, I want to take you out on a date. A real date."

She closed the distance and kissed him without even answering. She tasted like sweet tea and honey in his mouth. He didn't deepen the kiss. He let her take what she wanted and gave it right back. When she pulled away, she was slow to open her eyes.

"I'll let you take me out on a date when you remove the tracker from my car."

Mason grinned and pressed a quick kiss to her lips. "Not happening until I know you're safe. I've got to go pack."

"I would wish you good luck but…"

"Yeah, yeah, you already know." He kissed her cheek one last time before heading to the door. He glanced back once more. "Stay safe, Blue, and be sure to lock your door."

"Will do."

He opened the door and paused again turning around. "No matter what you find, promise me you'll wait until I get back."

She clasped her hands together and batted her eyes. "I promise to try."

Mason sighed. He knew exactly what that meant. Cree had a way of finding trouble or, rather, it finding her. His FBI interview couldn't have come at a worse time. He needed to be here. He needed to watch her back. "No more investigating without me. If you get a lead, you call me, and I'll have someone do the leg work until I get back and can do it myself."

He gave her that stern look that meant business, and she wiggled her fingers as he shut the door.

Chapter 12

My lips still tingled from our kiss as I locked the door behind Mason. He was an unexpected surprise I hadn't seen coming. Why hadn't I seen it coming? I'd have to ponder that later; albeit it *was* a nice surprise. I was leaning against the door reminiscing about the way he smiled at me when my phone rang.

"Hey, Cree. I've got an address on Mandy Stuart," Jitters said

"Perfect, text it to me. I'll go by her place after I visit Faraday in the hospital tomorrow. Tell Charlotte that I've got evidence and to call the rest of the gang in to meet tomorrow afternoon to use *Insight*."

"The twins are still out of town, but Winston should be back by then. I'll just need to check with the Doc to make sure he'll be available."

I loved these guys. The kind I could count on for anything. "Text me a time when you know for sure."

The rest of the night was uneventful as I hunkered down in front of the television trying to give my brain a rest. I needed the zone-out time and a good night's sleep as a way to reenergize before I used *Insight* tomorrow.

****

I woke rejuvenated and refreshed, ready to go. In no time I was stepping off the elevator onto Faraday's floor. I'd had to practically produce DNA in order to get past the watchdogs stationed at Faraday's door. Faraday knew me better than most people. He'd been there when I'd run away. Granted I was only five years old and made it only to my tree house, but he knew enough about me to know that I was stubborn. I could see it in his eyes as I approached the bed. The way he was taking me in as if he could read by look alone just how much trouble I'd managed to get into while he'd been under lock and key in the hospital bed.

"Detective Spencer told me that you were coming," he announced as I took his hand.

"Remind me not to invite Mason to any surprise parties." I kissed the stress wrinkles on Faraday's head.

"He also told me that you talked to Moreno."

I wasn't surprised. Leonard Mason Spencer had been on me like gum stuck to a shoe.

"Did he tell you that he put a tracker on my car?"

Faraday's lips twisted up into a grin. "No, but good for him. Someone has to keep you out of trouble."

"That's what everyone keeps telling me." I rolled my eyes and climbed up in the bed next to him as if I was about to read him a story. I was in a way. I was about to tell him the entire story of everything I'd been up to while he'd been resting.

When I was done, I could tell he was mulling over everything I'd uncovered. When the minutes ticked by, and I was sure he was about to yell, I spoke again. "Do you know what I don't get?"

"What's that, Cree?"

"The best friend, Mandy Stuart."

"Have you met her?"

"No, but if it were Charlotte who was missing and presumed dead, I don't think an entire army could stop me from trying to uncover the truth. I would have put out a full-page ad in the paper asking for leads. I would have wormed my way into every television talk show begging for clues or answers, and yet, I haven't seen or heard a peep from the best friend. Hell, I don't even know what she looks like yet and don't even get me started on the mysterious boyfriend. Some boyfriend he is."

"Sounds like you have more questions than answers."

"For now." I slid off the bed and took his hand again. "I've got your room ready at the Lady Blue when they release you."

"I hear you've been renting a new place next to the crime scene."

I grinned and shook my head. "He's a little tattletale."

"Stop being a pain in his ass, Cree. I asked him to watch out for you."

I let out a tired sigh. "I know." I kissed his forehead again. "Get some rest."

I was heading for the door when Faraday called out. "Hey, Blue."

I spun with my hand on the door.

"The librarian was dating Moreno's son, Mickey."

I let go of the door and walked back over to the bed. "Really? Moreno told me he'd never met the librarian."

"I couldn't find any connection, except the gun. Moreno's prints were on it. Mickey and his dad had a falling out when his mom died. Another suspicious death if you ask me."

"Mickey could have planted the gun."

Faraday shrugged. "I'm sure after you use *Insight*, you'll be able to tell me exactly what happened."

"I hope you're right." I patted his hand. "I'll keep you posted with what I find out."

I headed down to the lobby and found Freddie and George lounging on the chairs reading papers. I plopped down beside the bald ginormous Italian and crossed my legs. It was comical the way they shared a look with each other like I'd lost my mind.

"Did you need something?" Freddie asked.

"Yeah, actually I do. I need you guys to tell me where I can find Mickey Moreno."

"I'm afraid that isn't in our job description."

"Okay." I slapped my palms to my knees and rose from my seat. "I'm sure Moreno isn't going to be happy when I walk off his case." I held up my forefinger and thumb together an inch apart. "Especially when he was *this* close to being free."

I spun on my heels and headed out the electric doors and, for once in my life, thought maybe walking away from this case might be one of the wisest decisions I'd ever make.

I slipped inside my car just as the Freddie and George were getting into theirs. I waved once and pulled out, heading to the address that Jitters sent me for Mandy Stuart. If Frick and Frack didn't want to help me, maybe the best friend could point me in the right direction.

Fifteen minutes later I was parked on the street in front of a pizza parlor two blocks away from Main Avenue. I double-checked the address and noticed a darkened apartment upstairs and some side steps.

I climbed the stairs ignoring the grumble in my stomach and knocked on the door.

No answer, not even a sound coming from inside. I could wait. The smell from the pizzeria downstairs made my stomach growl louder. I'd still technically be waiting, if it was say, inside the pizza shop downstairs while stuffing my face. Who ever said stake outs were hard? This was a piece of cake, more like melted cheese pepperoni style pie. I chuckled as I jogged down the steps and headed inside.

The smell of hot and fresh pizza smacked me in the face with the garlicky homemade pizza sauce. The delicious scent was overpowering and calling my name. I had a bad habit of forgetting to eat when I was determined, but nothing could have dragged me away from the place before I had at least one slice except maybe the tenant arriving upstairs.

I sat at one of the stools at the counter and smiled at the man behind the counter.

"What can I get you?" he asked, pulling the pen from behind his ear.

"A slice of pepperoni and a sweet tea."

"That's it? Just one slice?" he asked, putting his pen back behind his ear without writing anything down.

"Afraid that's all I have time for. I was hoping to catch Mandy."

He raised his brow and wiped his hands on his apron before resting them on the counter. "Does Mandy know you're coming?"

Heat filled my cheeks. "Not quite, all I had was this address."

He gave a slow nod. "What's this about?"

"Margarete Stead."

I watched the suspicion in his eyes cross the rest of his face as a frown turned down at the corner of his lips. "Are you a cop?"

"Hey, Mickey, your order is up," one of the cooks yelled from the kitchen and rung the bell indicating an order was ready.

"You're the boyfriend," I whispered.

"What did you say?" he asked, turning the full force of his gaze back on me.

He had the same penetrating gaze as his father. The same color eyes and high cheekbones. "I didn't see the resemblance to

133

your dad, but I do now. You were Margarete's mysterious boyfriend. You're Mickey."

"Listen, lady, I don't know who you are—"

"She's helping your dad, kid. Tell her what she wants to know," Freddie answered as he and George took seats next to me.

"You don't look like the type of woman that hangs out with my dad."

I turned toward Freddie. "Is that a compliment?"

He nodded. "You've got brains instead of boobs. Take it."

"What do you want to know? I already told the cops what I knew."

"How did you meet Margarete?"

"I had a hook-up on MateSpace."

My mouth momentarily parted before I snapped it back closed. Mickey was a good-looking man. Tall, dark, and handsome and he owned his own restaurant. I could tell he did just by the décor and what was hanging on the walls. He had authentic Italian designs throughout. A picture of him and someone who appeared to be his grandmother or great-grandmother were posing in a picture in front of the building.

"You don't strike me as the type of guy that needs a dating site to meet women, and from everything I've heard about her, she doesn't strike me as the type of person to use those websites."

He ran his hand over his head while grabbing a slice of pizza from the case and sticking it in from of me. "Technically we didn't meet through MateSpace. I was meeting another woman at the library."

"Public place. I get it," I interjected. "Did that other woman ever show?"

"I don't know. I took one look at Margarete, and I knew I instantly that I was wasting my time even meeting with the other girl. Margarete..." He sighed, and his eyes turned sad. "She was beautiful. She had a kind soul, the kind you can actually see. Do you know what I mean?"

I did. "So you two just hit it off?"

"I've been with her ever since."

"Where were you that night she was shot and vanished?"

"Here, until close." He gestured toward the cameras high on the ceiling that point down to the registers. "The cops have video proof that I was here closing. We got a call in for six pizzas right before closing, so I stayed to help prep."

Goosebumps rose on my arms. He was telling the truth. I took a bite of the pizza and moaned. "This is good," I said around a mouthful of cheese.

"It's my great-grandma's recipe. God rest her soul."

I took a sip of my drink and swallowed. "Was Mandy upstairs the entire night?"

"How the hell would I know? Like I said, I was busy." His answer was short without elaborating.

No goosebumps. Huh.

"Any idea how your dad's gun was found on the scene?"

He shook his head. "My dad gave me a gun when I took over the pizza shop. He was worried about me working long hours and leaving at night. He's made a lot of enemies."

"You can't blame him, kid, with what happened to your mom."

"So it was your gun?" I asked, starting to get confused.

"Yeah. It was mine. I never even took it out of the box. I kept it in the storage room."

"Explains how your dad's prints were on the gun. He gave it to you, and you never touched it. Any idea how the gun got from here to Margarete's house?"

"Nope, but the restrooms are across from the storage area. I guess anyone could have slipped inside and taken it."

Goosebumps. Truth.

Who are you?" he asked again.

"Cree Blue. I own the Lady Blue Plantation just outside of town."

"You're the baker."

"No, she's not. She's the psychic who is helping your dad beat his charges." Freddie said loud enough for everyone in the entire place to hear.

All gazes around the counter and the tables next to it turned to stare at me.

"Actually I'm a bit of both, but it's supposed to be a secret," I answered in a whisper with a nudge toward the Neanderthal who had just shared it with everyone in the joint. So much for staying in the closet when a loud Italian knows your secrets. He was as bad as Mason about telling all my secrets. Maybe they should join a club, a let's-see-who-can-divulge-more club. "I have to ask." I paused for dramatic effect. "Do you know what happened to Margarete?"

"No."

No goosebumps. I frowned at his response and the lack of tingling feeling, which indicated he was telling the truth. He wasn't. He knew something.

I'd never gotten to question witnesses before. My goosebumps and sign for when I was being told the truth were coming in handy. I was like a human lie detector. Maybe I should add that to my business cards. That was something I'd have to ponder when I wasn't chasing ghosts.

"Did you love her?"

"God yes."

Goosebumps. Interesting.

"Is Moreno your dad?"

"I thought you already knew that."

Goosebumps.

"I did. I'm just testing a theory." I slid off my seat and pulled out my wallet.

Freddie was quick to drop some bills, but I stopped him. "It's not part of your job description."

I laid a twenty on the counter. "Do you know where I can find Mandy?"

"She lives upstairs, but I have no idea where she's at."

Not a single goosebump rose on my arm. Fibbing again. I tisked.

"Do you know where she works?"

"You might want to try the hospital. She's a nurse.

Goosebumps. Well, at least that part was true.

"Come to think of it, I remember her saying something about taking a vacation or something."

Not a single tingle on my skin. Liar

"How did Mandy come to live above your restaurant?"

"The place was vacant, and Mandy needed a place to live, so Margarete told her about it."

I turned to leave but stopped at the last minute. "Mickey, do you know where Margarete is?"

"No."

No goosebumps, not even a slight tingle or raised hair. Interesting, indeed. I would have asked him if he was sure since I knew he was lying, but I didn't want to tip him off that I was aware he lying. Evidence and or people could go missing; he was after all his father's son.

I walked out of the restaurant with more questions than the answers I'd been given.

DEAD WRONG

Chapter 13

I slid the phone out of my pocket and leaned back against my car while dialing Mason.

"Spencer," he barked into the phone.

"Mason, we weren't done. Who is that?" I heard the soft voice of a woman in the background catching me momentarily off guard.

"Hi, Mason, this is Cree. Is this a bad time?"

"Cree?" he asked seconds before I heard a door shut like he'd moved outside. "No, what's up?"

I paused, unsure what to say. Would a normal person ask about the woman? Probably not. I'd never be classified as normal.

"Are you married?" I just blurted it out very unlady-like.

"No... she's... a long story for another time." He sounded flustered. "Did you need something, Cree?"

"Uh, yeah. Sorry to bother you, but I need a favor."

"Where are you?"

"Outside Mickey Moreno's Pizzeria," I answered.

"Damn it, Cree. I told you no investigating."

"I was hungry." I answered and waved toward Moreno's henchmen, each eating a piece of pizza while they watched me from inside. "Listen. I have a gut feeling about Mickey."

"You think he killed her?"

"No." No way did a man that much in love kill his girlfriend. "But I think he knows where she is, or at least what happened."

"I read back through the reports after your neighbors mentioned a boyfriend. They'd already questioned Mickey, but I'll pick him up when I get back in town and question him again."

I hesitated. He wasn't going to like my next request. "That's not why I'm calling. I need to know where the tracker is on my car so I can put it on his."

The line went silent as if Detective Pissy Pants mulled it over. Seconds ticked by before he answered. "No. It stays on yours, and you need to just go home."

"Fine."

"I'm serious, Cree, go home."

I sighed, walking around my car to see if I could spot anything sticking out that didn't belong. No luck. "Have a great interview."

I didn't wait around for his reply before I hung up and slid into my car, not waiting on Tweedledee or Tweedledum. I'm sure they'd find me later.

The moon cast shadows on the road all the way back to the subdivision as my mind toyed with explanations why Mason might have a woman at his house this late at night when he'd told me he was packing to go out of town. She'd sounded a little irate in the background like I'd interrupted an argument. It would be just my dumb luck to be interested in a guy that was serious with someone else. I'd made the first move and kissed him. Stupid, stupid mistake. My mind replayed the conversation we'd just had and the one at my rental. I almost drove right by the subdivision sign. Braking at the last minute, I turned.

Lights danced behind curtains, and the streets were quiet and calm, with only one lady out walking her dog. I pulled up into my driveway and stared over at Margarete's dark empty house. "Tomorrow I'll know your secrets."

I headed inside. The package that Mason had left me was sitting on the counter. I poured a glass of wine and slipped onto a stool, staring at it in wonder of the secrets I'd soon uncover. I didn't dare open the package, not without the use of *Insight*. I wouldn't risk missing something important that could break this case wide open. Forgetting even the tiniest clue wasn't an option in this case, especially not when finding Faraday's shooter was involved.

I got that tingling feeling to expect a call, seconds before my cell phone vibrated, and I grabbed it checking the caller ID. Billson Correctional. "Hello."

"Lady Blue."

"This is Cree. Who is this?"

"Forget so soon? This is Dom Moreno."

I slid off my stool and headed for the back door to peer outside as if just talking to a criminal would make me guilty by association. "I haven't found her yet, but I'm getting close."

"So I hear," he answered.

I didn't even want to know how he knew what I was up to or what I'd found. "How is it you can call me without calling me collect?"

"Don't mind that. I found Faraday's shooter and before you start pointing fingers, no I didn't send them to do the job they took it upon themselves."

"Great give me a name."

"The shooter is being dealt with."

A string of apprehension coiled in my gut. Goosebumps rose on my arms. Truth.

"I never told you to deal with the guy. I just wanted his name."

"Relax, Cree. I said he's being dealt with, not that I put a hit on him. What kind of guy do you take me for?"

I wasn't touching that question, or I might find the next boots on my feet were plastered in concrete. Granted I'd manipulated him, threatened him, and coerced him into helping me, but I'd felt reasonably safe with him behind prison bars. I'm not sure I'd sleep so sound when he was released.

"What's his name, and where can I find him?"

"You can find out all about it on Channel 13 if you turn on the ten o'clock news."

I flipped on the television, but the news hadn't even started yet.

"I kept my end of the deal; now make sure you keep yours," Moreno said into the phone before the line went dead.

Grabbing my wine, I sat on the couch and turned up the volume. Within the next ten minutes, there was a news conference on the steps of the police station. A picture of a dark Italian was in the corner of the screen.

The police chief started to speak as the crowd of reporters quieted down. "Mark Manicello has turned himself into authorities and has confessed to being the trigger man who shot veteran Detective John Faraday. That is all we have at this time."

I watched as the reporters bombarded the chief with questions he either couldn't answer or wouldn't. The man in the picture had that kind of hard look about him. Tattoos covered his neck and arms, and an old scar ran down the side of his face. He was the type of guy you'd cross the street to get away from.

My phone rang again, and I checked the caller ID. Mason. Butterflies still danced in my stomach, even though I was hesitant to find out who that other woman might be. "Hello."

"Did you see the news?"

"Yep. Moreno called and told me to watch it. He said he kept his end of the bargain. I'm still in shock."

"That makes two of us."

"How do you think Moreno convinced him to turn himself in?"

"I'm sure the guy was more scared of what Moreno might do to him than what he'll face in jail. I warned you, Cree, these are bad people."

Everyone had been warning me that Moreno was the head cheese. Had I really gotten all this wrong? He might not have been the one to pull the trigger since he was with a mysterious blonde, but he was extremely capable of having a hit placed on the librarian's head. Crap. No. I shook my head. My feelers and goosebumps had never been wrong. Would this be the first time? "I heard your message loud and clear."

"Cree... about earlier."

I stopped him mid-sentence. "It's okay. You don't owe me an explanation. It's not like we're dating. Heck, I kissed you first. I should have asked if you were in a relationship or serious with someone else."

"I kissed you back, and besides, I'm not, not in the way you think."

I lowered my head and closed my eyes. "Good luck, Mason."

Two additional glasses of wine later, and I could barely keep my eyes open. I had a busy day tomorrow, taking the librarian's evidence to the plantation to find out once and for all what had really happened to the missing woman. I triple-checked my locks and headed for bed.

Chapter 14

There was never a good reason to wake up before eight in the morning. It has always been my motto that the early bird can keep the worm. Tuning in beneath the veil always drained me and kept me a hard sleeper on most nights.

I'm not sure what woke me as I rested my hand over my heart to calm the beats. The room was familiar enough in a woman-was-murdered-next-door kind of way and the place I'd been calling home for the last week or so. Closing my eyes, I strained to hear anything or anyone out of place, and I was met with silence. Pure, unnatural silence, the deafening kind, where you all you can hear is the sound of your breath escaping your lips.

The sound of my doorbell broke the silence the same time I got the tingling feeling a call was coming in. I threw the covers to the side letting them land in a heap on the floor the second my cell rang. Stumbling over the covers, I ignored my cell and wiped the sleep from my eyes while making my way to the door. I unlocked the deadbolt, grumbling beneath my breath. Whoever was outside needed to be the taught the proper etiquette for an appropriate time to visit.

I peered behind the curtains to find news vans parked on the street and reporters standing outside. Irritation coiled down my spine as I yanked the door open. "Do you guys have any idea of the time?"

I was greeted by blinding flashes and microphones shoved in my face.

"Sources say that you're working to get Moreno out of jail. Is there any validity to that claim, and if so, how do you plan to get him out?" someone asked.

"Do you see more than ghosts? Does the rest of the Blue family have your abilities?"

"Why are you living in the Shady Oak Subdivision when you own a plantation?"

"How long have you been working with the police department, and which cases are you responsible for solving?"

The reporters' questions came fast and clipped like the flashes that continued. Neither broke the haze that covered my mind as I tried to make sense out of what was going on.

"Uh…" I stared around at all of my neighbors out in their yards and sorted through the faces of the people on my stoop. One face stood out, and judging by the scowl on her face, Ava was none too happy by what she was hearing. I'd be lucky if my lease wasn't revoked. "No comment."

I shut the door and locked it. Pressing my back up to the wood, I clenched my eyes closed. Where in the heck had they gotten that their information? I hurried back through the house and grabbed my phone to find I had four missed calls, all from Charlotte. I listened to the first one as I headed into the bathroom. Her words faded out as I stared at my reflection in the mirror. My hair was standing on end and in tangles. The mascara and eyeliner I'd forgotten to take off was smudged down my face like I'd gotten drunk last night and stayed out partying. I looked like a psychotic mess, and now everyone in Billson would have a good laugh at my expense if they were laughing at all. I was probably the most hated person in town with the way they portrayed me helping a criminal.

Technically I was, but only because he was innocent of the crime that had gotten him locked up.

I hit replay on my messages. "Cree, you need to call me," Charlotte said.

The second was a bit more urgent. "We have a problem, call me back."

The third she was on the verge of hysterics. "Reporters are camped outside the Lady Blue gate."

In the fourth, her voice trembled. "Feds showed up at the Lady Blue wanting to ask you some questions. I told them you weren't here, but they left a card. They want you to call them. Cree, what the hell is going on? What did you do?"

I hopped in the shower. The entire time I was playing over different ways that I could get out of the house without detection. If reporters were camped outside and at the Lady Blue, there was only one other way onto that property, through dark spider-infested stone tunnels that my ancestors had built during one of the wars. I shivered at the thought.

A plan started to form in my mind, one that could end this for good. It was risky, but it was the best shot I had. I hurried to dry my hair and changed into respectable clothes and grabbed the evidence bag that Mason had brought over. Letting out a shaky breath, I pulled open the door to find all the reporters talking amongst themselves next to their news vans.

They clamored with their cameras and video equipment as they ran again into the yard. I smiled sweetly at each of them and held the bag firmly in my grasp before clearing my throat.

"Thank you each for coming. I know what I do is unorthodox, and many may not believe in what I can do, but the truth is I sometimes help work on cold cases."

"Is it true that you're helping to get Moreno out of jail?"

I shrugged. "He's innocent of this crime."

"But not countless others," one called out.

"I'm not a cop." I let my gaze run over each of them. "I'm sure if he's responsible for anything, the police are working hard to find the evidence to prove it. However, in the case of the Margarete Stead, I believe the police got it wrong, and that means there is still some diabolical killer out on the loose. If I can help, I feel it's my civic duty to see that the correct person is brought to justice."

"Who is the correct person?" the reporter standing closest to me asked before shoving her microphone in my face.

I smiled and stared into the camera, holding up the package in my hand. "I'm hoping to have more information in the next twenty-four hours. Thank you."

They were still shouting out questions as I pushed through the crowd toward my Jeep. One of the tires was half deflated, and all the bravado I'd just shown in front of the camera escaped out on a sigh. Ava was standing next to her husband on the sidewalk across the street. He had a phone pressed to his ear, and Ava had her fist rested on her hip. She pegged me with her glare as a hand landed on my arm, making me jump.

"Looks like you could use a lift," Marcie announced and led me across the lawn to her car. "Lucky for you I have a new car." She clicked the fob and slid in behind the wheel and buckled her belt. "You wouldn't have been able to get out anyway. They're blocking your drive."

She backed out of her drive and sped down the street while glancing in the rearview mirror. "They don't know this subdivision like I do."

"Have you lived here long?"

"Not long at all."

I kept glancing over my shoulder, and within the first five minutes, I had no idea where we were, but there was no one following behind us. Marcie pulled into a parking garage and backed up into a parking space. "Was there somewhere you want me to drop you?"

The thought of going to the plantation and dealing with more reporters was the last thing I wanted to do. Maybe if I stayed out of sight for a while the news crews would all go away or find another more interesting story to report. Charlotte was probably blocked in at the plantation, Mason was on his way to Washington, and heck, I didn't even have the numbers for Tweedledee or Tweedledum. Craptastic. I yanked on the door handle and pushed it open.

"I'll manage. Thanks for your help and I'm sorry about the trouble."

"No trouble. I think it's cool that you're psychic."

On days like this, that made one of us. I smiled and shut the door and headed back out of the parking garage. I hit the sidewalk and glanced both ways and immediately knew where I was. The mail drop box I liked to use across town to send my special letters from was just across the street. Two men in suits were standing in front of it. One was gesturing to the camera on the outside of the post office building while holding a picture in his hand.

The other man was staring at me. He nudged the other suit in the arm and nodded his head in my direction.

"Ms. Blue," he called out, and they both started jogging across the street as Marcie pulled out of the garage.

I hugged the evidence package tighter to my chest as they stopped in front of me. The other one spoke. "Cree Blue?"

"Yes," I answered, trying hard not to let my flight instinct kick in.

The man who said my name pulled out a badge and flashed it at me. "I'm FBI Special Agent Samuel Hunter, and this is Special Agent Rick Fernandez. We'd like to ask you some questions."

"How can I help you, gentlemen?"

"We'd like you to come with us," Hunter said, like it was more of a demand than a request.

"I don't mean to be rude, but now isn't the best time. Can we do this later?"

Hunter glanced at Fernandez. Neither one of them seemed amused.

Fernandez pulled his phone out of his pocket and hit a button. "Sir, we have her."

I took a tentative step back. Not that I'd be able to outrun these guys, not even on a good day. The last time I'd been on a treadmill was when I had a gym membership. That expired ten years ago.

Fernandez held out his phone, and I paused in my tracks. "Take it."

I shook my head. I didn't want to know who was on the other end.

"Take it."

"No."

"Yes." He pegged me with his glare and shoved the phone to my ear before releasing it.

I barely caught it in time and moved it back to where I could hear. "Hello?"

"Ms. Blue?"

I didn't recognize the voice on the other end of the line. It was deep and scratchy and held an air of authority. I bet this man, just based on the tone of his voice, wasn't used to hearing no. "Yes."

"You were very good, but we're better."

"Story of my life, pal. Could you be a bit more cryptic?" My brows dipped, and I glanced at the phone. The display read Deputy Director Harrison Reed, and I knew instantly that any choices I thought I had were slowly disappearing like the veggies on my plate when I was ten. Too bad the dog wasn't around to turn this phone into a new chew toy.

"Director Reed." I covered the receiver. "We go way back," I whispered to Fernandez and Hunter. "How's Glenys? Did you catch her stalker and find his secret lair where I told you to look?"

"You single-handedly gave us what we needed to arrest him for three murders. The sick asshole kept mementos of each woman he terrorized before killing them. But he won't be harming anyone else, and Glenys is safe thanks to you."

I slowly started to pace. "I'm glad to hear it. Not many people would act on an anonymous tip. That's what it was you know... anonymous."

He chuckled into the phone. "You almost stayed anonymous, but you forgot one thing."

"Oh?"

"Each post office scans the address in a code on the envelope so the origin and destination can be tracked. It's all automated."

I hadn't thought of that. Dang it. I spun around to the post office and shook my head. "That brought you here, but how did you know I was the person who sent the letter?"

"Did you know that Billson Police Department has the highest success rate of solved cold cases in a three-state radius?"

"Maybe I need to expand my geography."

"Dating as far back as 1952."

I grinned. I knew my dad was good, but damn. I had no idea they kept statistics on it. I chuckled. "I guess I can't take all the credit. I wasn't even born then."

"Poke the right people, and you'll eventually get answers. It didn't hurt we obtained surveillance from the post office with what you were wearing. When the agents looked at the surveillance from the parking garage, we traced your license plate."

Dang it. I thought I'd been so careful, so meticulous. I might as well have been holding up a freakin sign saying come get me. "I'm guessing you didn't just call to thank me?"

"Technically, yes. I owe you, Ms. Blue. But I do have another proposition for you."

My brows lifted, and I stopped pacing. "Oh?"

"Off the books of course."

I rolled my eyes. "Is there any other way with you people?"

"I need your help to solve a thirty-year-old murder."

Murder, cold case. Now the man was talking a language I understood. "Don't tell me any more information. Just send me something personal of the victim's from the evidence box, and I'll let you know what I get."

"Excellent. I'll have it hand-delivered by the end of the week."

I was about to hand back the phone when I paused. "Oh, one more thing."

"Yes?"

"Mason Spencer is interviewing for a position with your agency. Do yourself a favor, and hire him."

"Ms. Blue, we have strict guidelines on who we hire. There's a process involved."

"Cree," I was quick to amend. "Trust me. It would be like winning the lottery. He was trained by the best, and he was one of the few that believed me when push came to shove."

"I'll see what I can do."

"Thanks, Harrison"

"Director Reed," he amended.

Funny man. He might not know it yet, but one day he'd be pushy, wanting me to call him Harrison. Some things I just knew. This was one of them. There were people that were meant to be in my life; souls we keep in our circles that we move from one life to another. Harrison was a part of my soul family, even if he didn't know it. "Oh, I do need one other favor."

"Name it."

"Do you think your agents can get me into the plantation without having to be bombarded by media and then over to my rental place? Maybe if they used their badges, it might scare some of those pushy reporters off. I'll call us even for you not letting me stay anonymous."

Harrison chuckled. "Is that all you want, a ride?"

"From these two very intimidating men, yes."

"Of course. It's the least I can do. Put Fernandez on the phone."

I grinned as I held the phone out to Fernandez. "Take it."

Chapter 15

Well, going to the plantation had been a bust. The others who normally helped me work *Insight* were either intimidated by the media presence or just busy, kind of like the doctor who would help me connect. It was just my luck. I locked up the evidence bag and had the feds escort me to my rental. The streets were eerily calm. No reporters or vans were sitting around waiting to jump me as I got out of the SUV.

"Do you need us to walk you in?"

I dangled my key. "Nope. I think I can handle it from here. It looks like the press got tired of waiting."

Both guys pulled out business cards and handed them to me. "We've been ordered to escort you wherever you need to go while we're here."

"Really?" I asked with hope in my voice. Maybe having the FBI personally chauffeuring me around might make a murderer think twice about trying to take me out before I revealed his name.

"We're leaving tomorrow at three."

I had them for less than twenty-four hours. I sighed. "Thanks, guys."

I got out of the SUV and waved, giving them a salute before making it to my door. A pest control notice was taped to the wood, along with a little note from the realtor saying she'd let them in. It was scheduled for service and part of my lease. Guess I should have read the fine print and at least amended it to read, "not when a killer is out to get me."

Shoving my key into the lock, I ripped the notice from the door and walked inside, turning the lock behind me. I reached for a light two seconds after I saw the dark figure sitting in the corner. A scream bubbled from my throat, momentarily freezing me in place.

"It's just me," Faraday announced, making my heart beat again.

I flicked on the lights. "Were you trying to give me a heart attack? Because you almost succeeded."

The look on his face wasn't one of those that a godfather would give his goddaughter, similar to a grandparent in whose eyes you could never do anything wrong. No...this was more like a cop's or parent's scrutiny, as though I'd stayed out past curfew and come home nine months pregnant. This disapproving look did nothing for his stress lines.

"Grammy always said if you keep frowning, your face is going to freeze like that."

His lips twitched. I didn't even get a partial smile. The silence lingered, from his end anyway.

"What are you doing here, big cheese?" My favorite nickname for him, and it just so happened to be the one he hated most. I figured if I wasn't going to get any type of emotional response, maybe pissy might be better than silent.

"You've got a target on your back." His voice was gruff, and he winced trying to climb out of the chair with his left arm still in a sling.

"I couldn't help the media. They just showed up here. I'm sure the killer wouldn't chance showing up when the media had just been camped out on my lawn." I headed into the kitchen to grab him an aspirin and some water.

"You publicly announced you're helping Moreno beat his charges. I'm afraid there are more people gunning for you than just the murderer. One guy I could fight, but rumor on the street is you pissed off a bunch of people. Everyone from normal citizens to my brothers in blue who you're making sound incompetent."

"Well, if the shoe fits," I whispered beneath my breath. "Who dropped you off? I didn't see your car outside."

This time he let out a full grin. "The realtor snuck me in with the cover of pest control. Five of us showed up, and only four of us left."

"Sneaky, I like it." I handed him the water and pill. "You should be at the hospital or at least at the Lady Blue resting."

"I got a visit today from the feds." He lifted a salt and pepper brow in my direction. "Then Mason called. He was worried."

I folded my arms across my chest and Faraday's gaze followed. I quickly unfolded them. Folded arms meant I was being defensive. Hell, even I knew that. I headed back into the kitchen and grabbed a bottle of wine and a glass and poured. "I'm surprised he found time to call, with him going out of town and the woman staying at his place."

I sipped my wine watching Faraday for any tell-tale sign. I don't know what I was looking for, but turnabout was fair play.

"I didn't peg you for being a jealous type."

"I'm not jealous," I amended and sat on the couch, sliding my feet beneath my body. "Grammy taught me better than to play with married or unavailable men. I'm just surprised my guides didn't warn me."

"He isn't married," Faraday answered, easing back down in the chair he'd been holed up in when I arrived. "But it's complicated. He and his girlfriend have a kid together. They were high school sweethearts, and he still helps her out from time to time. Kind of like now. He took them in because a fire destroyed their house. They had nowhere to go."

My heart sank at the thought. Rekindling old flames would be easy to accomplish if sharing the same roof. "That's horrible."

"They stayed friends for his daughter's benefit, and he's just a nice guy. He'd never turn down anyone in need of help."

I felt like a heel. Deep down I knew Mason was a good man, but he had a daughter with this woman. I was beginning to feel like Suzie Home-wrecker. "You're in no condition to be playing babysitter."

"I came prepared." He slid his gun out of his arm sling and showed it to me before sliding it back inside. He winced, and sweat beaded his brow.

No matter what he said, the only place he needed to be was back at the hospital, being pampered by some cute nurses. He couldn't convince me otherwise. "I'll make you a deal. I'll let you stay but on one condition."

"I don't make deals," he announced.

I sighed and slipped my phone from my pocket. "Does your brass know you've skipped out of the hospital?"

"You wouldn't."

"My dad and Grammy would expect no less."

"What's your deal?"

"You can stay, but you're sleeping on my bed. I'll sleep on the couch."

"Absolutely not," he grumbled and pushed himself out of the chair with a little more zest than I'd expected.

"Maybe I need to call my new FBI friends to take you back to the hospital." I held up both cards and waved them with a smile on my face. I rose from my spot and dropped the cards onto the table. "Come on, let's get you settled in."

"I can't protect you from the bedroom."

"Oh, trust me, old man. You'll hear my scream if some intruder decides to kill me in the middle of the night."

An hour later, I'd changed into my nightclothes and had already made up the couch with a blanket and pillow in hopes this would all be over soon.

My phone vibrated on the table, and I grabbed it and answered, keeping my voice low as not to wake up Faraday. "Hello."

"Hey, Cree. It's Mason. I just wanted to check in with you."

"I'm fine," I answered, walking over to the curtain and peering outside. Moreno's Tweedledee and Tweedledum were bent down by my Jeep in the dark and looked to be fixing my tire. "Are you nervous about your interview?"

"Nervous, no. It's one of my goals but interview couldn't have come at a worse time. I left you in the middle of this just when the media found out about what you're trying to do. You need someone watching your back."

"Moreno's men are fixing my tire as we speak."

"Cree." He sighed.

"Is that why you called Faraday to babysit me?"

"I didn't call Faraday. I've been on a plane. Is he there? Let me talk to him." Mason's voice turned demanding in that type of way cops ask for your driver's license after pulling you over for speeding. Of course, I wouldn't know, but I'd heard.

I let the curtain drop and turned to find Faraday standing behind me. He had a gun pointed at my back.

"Tell him you have to go, Cree, or he's next." Faraday gestured to the phone.

"He can't talk right now." My voice trembled as I tried to keep it together. "He's sleeping. We'll talk later."

I acted like I hung up the phone and set it on the table. "What are you doing, Faraday? Why are you pointing your gun at me?"

"I can't let you do it," he said as sweat beaded his brow.

I held up my hands. "Do what? I haven't done anything."

"You've made a mess out of everything, Cree. I can't let you find a loophole for Moreno to use to get out of jail. He's scum, and he deserves to stay behind bars."

"He didn't kill the librarian."

"We have evidence that says otherwise." I slowly started to inch backward toward my front door.

"I'm telling you he didn't. What are you going to do, shoot me?" I screamed at the top of my lungs, hoping Mason or the muscle outside might hear. I wouldn't be one of the unsolved cases. I'd probably be another one they tried to pin on Moreno or one of his guys, but I wasn't going down without a fight.

"You shouldn't have stuck your nose where it doesn't belong."

"I did that for you!" I screamed. "To find the shooter that almost killed you... and this...." My eyes pleaded only because this man was supposed to be my godfather.

"You made a deal with the devil."

I pressed my back to the door, quietly unlocking the locks.

"Did you kill the librarian and plant the evidence to charge Moreno?"

"Hell no. I've never planted evidence. That stroke of luck fell into my lap."

"I had to ask," I said, slowly twisting the knob behind my back. "You're about to kill an innocent person."

"You don't understand. I'm not going to get the chance to arrest him again. He needs to stay locked up. I'm saving hundreds of lives."

"By taking mine?" I asked, twisting the knob in my hand.

He moved closer to me and cocked the trigger, making it difficult for me to breathe. My entire body was frozen, my mind useless. I was about to die by hands that helped raise me.

"I'll make it quicker than Moreno will," he whispered between us.

His words registered. His body was so close. Although he was old, he still had me at gunpoint, and that would always trump my advantage of youth.

I let out a shaky breath. "You were supposed to take care of me." I shook my head as anger seeped in my soul. "You were like a father to me. You were supposed to protect me," I growled my words loud and in his face.

His brows dipped. My words were sinking in. Right before I rammed my forehead into his, sending him reeling backward and down to his knees.

Grammy always told me to use my wits in the event of a fight. I'm not sure she meant my actual head, but it worked. I spun around and had the door open two seconds before I heard the gun go off behind me. I darted around the bushes and out of the line of sight.

Freddie and George were nowhere to be seen. I had no phone; I had no keys. I had no way to escape. I didn't even stop to glance over my shoulder as I headed to Marcie's door and started ringing the doorbell. No one answered.

"Crap." I was heading for her neighbor when a pair of arms snagged out and caught me, pulling me between the houses. A scream bubbled from my lips.

"Shh. I've got you." I recognized the Italian accent as George immediately.

"What are you doing out here?" I whispered.

"I was looking for Freddie. We were watching from down the street, and we saw someone slipping between houses. Freddie left to investigate but never returned."

"Come out, Cree," Faraday yelled. "Let's talk about this."

My entire body trembled as George shoved me behind his back and slowly started inching down the side of the house toward the back. He grabbed my hand and ran toward the storage shed behind Marcie's. He yanked open the door and shoved me inside the dark space.

"Stay here."

"I'll be trapped."

"Find a place to hide and keep your head down. I'll take care of the cop."

"Please don't hurt him. Just knock him out or something." I nodded and backed away so he could shut the door.

George shook his head and shut the door. I didn't want Faraday to die. He'd been like a father. Something wasn't right with him or what he was doing, but I'd never forgive myself if he died because of me.

The sound of moaning had me spinning around when an overhead light flicked on. Freddie was tied up on the ground with a piece of tape over his mouth. Marcie had the barrel of her gun pointed at me.

"That goon hand-delivered you to me." Marcie chuckled as she took a step in my direction.

"You?" I shook my head in disbelief.

"Of course me." She seethed through gritted teeth and gestured to the ground next to Freddie. "Mickey should have been mine, but that whore stole him before he even met me."

I shared a look of understanding with Freddie as I lowered to my knees next to him. "You were his MateSpace hook up at the library?"

"I was, but my damn car wouldn't start. I followed her one day from the library. It was pure luck the house next door was for rent. I knew she deserved to die for taking what was supposed to be mine."

This woman was freakin' delusional. I'd walked, well, really ran from one person who wanted to kill me straight into the path of another. "What did you do with Margarete?"

"I got her good. I shot her just like I'm going to do to both of you. She got away from me. I chased her into the woods behind the park. She lost a lot of blood. I'm sure her dead body is rotting in there."

"What if she's not?" My hands were shaking. "She isn't dead. I'm psychic. I would know."

"You're lying," she growled. "I wore a mask and gloves. She'd never be able to guess it was me. I took the diamond ring that Mickey gave her as a memento. That diamond was meant for my finger, not that snooty bitch's. It was so easy to steal the gun from the pizza shop. Hell, it still had the gift tag attached. Planting Moreno's gun was pure genius. I had to." Her eyes turned wild. "I can't have him ruining mine and Mickey's life. He deserves to rot in jail."

This was starting to make sense. Mickey's lies were starting to make sense. He'd lied when I asked if he knew where Margarete was. He did know because he was fucking protecting her from this psychotic bitch.

A smile slowly split my lips. If I was going to die, I was going to take Marcie's dreams with me. "She's alive."

Marcie's eyes narrowed to slits as Freddie tried to sit up next to me. "Stop lying."

I shook my head. "Her best friend is a nurse; her boyfriend is the son of a mob boss. All you did was drive them closer together. She got away from you that night and ran right into her lover's arms. I bet they've already started trying to make little Mickey Juniors."

Marcie raised her gun and aimed at my head and pulled the trigger. Freddie jumped in front of my body, taking the hit, and slumped to the floor. I charged Marcie like a bull in a china shop. No way was I letting Freddie take my shot and I not take this bitch down.

Marcie had made a mistake. She hadn't tried to subdue me. She probably thought I was a southern belle who couldn't land a punch. Nothing was further from the truth.

I lowered my shoulder and charged her in the gut, knocking the gun out of her hand as we both flew backward against a shed full of crap. My head smacked against the post of a shovel as she tumbled into a wheelbarrow. I grabbed the shovel and held it to her throat like a snake I'd killed at the Lady Blue plantation.

The door to the shed burst open. Two cops and the two FBI agents that had given me a ride were standing at the entrance.

"She's trying to kill me," Marcie cried.

Special Agent Fernandez walked into the shed and took the shovel out of my hands.

"How did you know I was in trouble?"

"We were having dinner with the police chief when Detective Spencer called."

"We heard the gunshot and found Faraday unconscious," Special Agent Hunter added. "EMS has him, and then he'll be booked."

Fernandez grabbed Marcie out of the wheelbarrow. Her demands I be arrested were going unheard as they slapped the cuffs on her.

"Freddie saved my life. He's been shot. We need to get him to a hospital."

Hunter snapped his fingers, and the other cops moved out of the way for a stretcher to enter.

I held Freddie's hand. Not because he needed it. This probably wasn't even his first bullet wound, but I needed it. I smiled down at him. "Taking a bullet for me wasn't part of your job."

"It is now. I'll be seeing you, Blue." He coughed, and blood spurted from his lips as the paramedics wheeled him away.

DEAD WRONG

Chapter 16

After giving my statement, and within the hour, the whole neighborhood was infested with police cars and men combing the area and inside Marcie's house. Several of the forensic team members walked out with bags. One contained a black mask and gloves, and another had a bag with a diamond ring in one hand and a bag with a gun in the other.

I'd been taken to the hospital and checked for a concussion before being released. I asked the nurse for Freddie's room and took the elevator up to the third floor. I slowly opened the door. Freddie was lying on the bed with his eyes closed. Mickey was in the room, along with a woman wearing a hat and a nurse checking Freddie's vitals. I didn't need *Insight* to tell me who they were.

"You must be Margarete and Mandy," I said as I stepped inside and let the door close behind me.

All eyes turned and met mine.

"I couldn't tell you she was alive. We didn't know who'd tried to kill her," Mickey said.

"I know," I answered and walked to the bed to peer down at Freddie. "I think it's time Margarete rises from the dead. Your dad is sitting in jail for killing her."

"That's where we're going next."

Margarete rounded the bed and took my hands. "I'm sorry you got involved. I didn't want anyone else to get hurt. I planned to show up in court, to tell the truth about being alive. I wouldn't have let Mickey's dad take the fall. I just couldn't, not yet. I was too scared."

I squeezed her hand. "I'm just glad you're okay."

I answered with all honesty, even though my heart was shattered into a million pieces. Margarete would eventually heal from this ordeal. I'm not sure I ever would.

"We're in your debt," Mickey announced.

I shook my head and glanced at Freddie. "I'm in his."

I headed out of the room with one last look at Freddie on the bed. I'd find a way to repay him for saving my life. I had to.

I headed down to the lobby to find both FBI agents lounging in chairs. Fernandez was on his phone and quickly snapped it closed and rose as I neared. "We leave you alone for an hour, and you're almost killed."

I shrugged. "But I wasn't."

"No, you weren't." Special Agent Hunter gestured to the automatic doors. "We figured you might need a ride."

I laughed, contradicting a tear that slipped free.

****

It took a week for the buzz of reporters to disappear and almost everything to return to the new version of normal. I slid my hands down my black dress as I stared in the mirror. The color in my cheeks had yet to return. I felt like I was going to a funeral, and in some ways, I was.

"Are you ready?" Charlotte asked, leaning against the doorframe.

"As ready as I'll ever be," I answered and followed her downstairs where Mason was pulling at his tie while waiting with Faraday's attorney and the chief of police.

"Are you sure you want to do this?" Mason asked, holding my gaze.

I nodded and gestured to the library and let Charlotte lead the way.

"Ms. Blue." The chief nodded in passing as he entered the room. The attorney remained silent, and who could blame him? He had no idea what I was about to say or do.

I waited for everyone to be seated. The energy in the air was thick with uncertainty. I'm sure several more feelings would soon be added to that mixture before I was done.

"Thank you all for coming." I took a seat behind my father's desk, hoping to soak up some of his lingering courage. Grammy and Mother were in the corner of the room watching me. No one could see them but me, but it was another form of support I needed today.

"What's this about?" the chief asked, letting his gaze go from Mason's back to mine.

"I'd like to make a deal."

The attorney glanced at the chief and then back at me. "What kind of deal?"

"I'll drop the charges against John Faraday on one condition."

The chief narrowed his eyes, and the attorney's ears perked up.

"What condition?" Faraday's attorney asked.

"John Faraday has been a friend to my family all my life and even before it. He was the only man who believed in my father's abilities and also mine."

"He tried to kill you, Ms. Blue," the chief butted in.

"I don't believe he was in his right mind or that he would have followed through. I have it on good authority that if you were to check the ceiling of the rental house, that you'll find the bullet that was discharged. The gun wasn't aimed at me when he fired. We both know that without it, the District Attorney doesn't have a case, and Internal Affairs can't do much but potentially suspended him for discharging his weapon. As far as the threats he made, those would be up to me if I felt the need to press charges."

"Cree." Mason rose from his seat and started pacing the room behind the couches. "I heard him threaten to kill you with my own ears."

I nodded. Everything Mason said was true. I couldn't deny that. "John has been after Moreno for longer than I've been alive. He was on medication, and to be honest, I don't think he was going to kill me."

"You did at the time," Mason answered, crossing his arms over his chest. "I heard it in your voice."

I let out a long sigh and leaned back. "Sure, he wanted to scare me, but we both know that if he intended to kill me, that bullet he fired wouldn't have missed his target. He's a crack shot, always has been."

"What's your condition?" the attorney asked with the pen poised over his legal pad.

"For starters, I'd like him to get counselling to deal with his anger toward Moreno. It's neither natural nor healthy. He's almost at retirement. One *almost*"—I used quote marks when I spoke the word to punch home my point —"bad deed doesn't make him a bad man. He's done so much good, not just for my family but for the citizens of this town. He doesn't deserve to be locked up with criminals. I just think he momentarily snapped. He'd lost his home. Hell, he was almost killed. Things like that can really mess with a person's head."

"We accept," the counselor was quick to announce.

"I wasn't done," I said, rising from my chair. "I'd like you to give him back his job."

"Now that's out of the question," the police chief said. "Don't get me wrong, I like Faraday, and up until this incident he was a good cop, but I can't trust him."

I nodded in complete understanding. I truly did understand. "His retirement is in a couple months. I'm not asking you to put him on active cases but to work as a liaison between me and the cold cases I was helping to solve. Consider it community service. He understands how I work, and you still get the benefit of my help. He'll live here…"

Mason walked out of the room, stealing the rest of my sentence when everyone turned to watch him leave. I cleared my throat to regain attention. "He's homeless. He'll live here after he attends counselling and until the therapist believes he's not a threat."

"Why would you even offer that?" the Chief asked.

"He's family. He'll always be my family." A tear slid down my cheek just as my dad appeared in the room. He smiled, and I almost lost it. I took a deep breath and smiled back. "When he reaches retirement, he'll be free to leave or whatever he wants. Those are my terms for dropping the charges."

"You can't be serious," the chief demanded.

"Saving Faraday was the whole reason I went into this case, and I'm going to damn sure finish what I started."

"He's not going to agree."

"You're probably right." I shrugged. It was always a possibility that the guilt from what he'd almost done would eat him alive. He was hard-headed when he wanted to be. "But I have to try."

The chief's face softened, something I never thought I'd live long enough to see. "You truly believe that he wouldn't have harmed you?"

I glanced to my family's spirits in the corner. "I have it on good authority that he just wanted to scare me, to push home the point that what I was doing was dangerous." I met the chief's gaze. "Will you let him be the liaison and help all of us bring peace to the families from your cold cases?"

The chief ran his hand over his head. "You drive a hard bargain."

"Think of all the families you'll be helping."

He nodded. "After his counselling, if I'm satisfied with the therapist's reports that he's making progress, then I'll agree."

A smile eased on my lips as I turned to the attorney. "Those are my terms."

"He'll accept. I'll see to it."

"Not that I don't trust you," I said, sliding the top drawer open. I pulled out the letter I'd written to Faraday. It was short, sweet, and to the point.

I love you. I forgive you for trying to scare sense into me, and it's time to come home and help me solve these cold cases. I'll have the cookies waiting.

"Give him this, and when he agrees, you and the Chief can make the necessary arrangements."

In the next thirty minutes, I had everyone out of the house and was surprised to find

Mason's car still in my drive. I walked back inside and went in search to find him standing at the kitchen counter next to the cookies. The sight made me smile.

"I needed a few minutes before I started to yell. I followed the smell of your cookies. They seemed to calm me down."

"I'll have to remember that." I grinned and went to the plate and handed him two while I nibbled on one. "I know you don't believe I know what I'm doing, but honest, I do."

He chewed and swallowed before he answered. "I'll never understand you."

I chuckled. He wasn't the first. "Congrats on the new job."

"How did you know?" he asked, his brows dipped.

"I have friends in high places," I said, walking to the fridge. I poured us both a glass of milk and set them next to the cookies. I dunked mine, and he looked like I should be arrested for doing it.

"This is a good opportunity for me," he announced, setting his cookie down. He took my hand.

"I know. It's your dream." I smiled up at him. "You've got to take it."

"This isn't the end between us," he said, kissing my cheek.

"I know. You promised me a date when you got back." I grinned.

"My daughter lives here."

I smiled. "I know. I heard you had one."

Mason chuckled. "Faraday told you."

I nodded.

"I'll be back often to see her." He cupped my cheek and leaned down to stare into my eyes. "And you."

He pressed his lips to mine in a kiss that only lovers would share. Not that we were, but we were defiantly headed in that direction. One day at a time. That was all any of us really had.

My doorbell rang, breaking the moment. "Sorry."

"It's okay. I have to leave." He followed me to the door, standing right next to me as I pulled it open.

My mouth parted, and words escaped me.

"Blue," Freddie said, smiling down at me. "You're a rock star."

I gave a full-belly laugh. "Hardly, what are you doing here, and who's your friend?"

"I've decided to make you my full-time protection detail since you're going to be running around chasing criminals." Freddie pointed his thumb at the man next to him. "And I don't know who this guy is, but if you want, I can get rid of him."

"Or I can," Mason announced.

My brows dipped. "Wait, what?"

The man standing next to him held out his hand. "Ms. Blue, I'm West Archer. I believe FBI Deputy Director Reed told you I'd be coming."

His delicious British accent caught me momentarily off guard.

"Yes of course. Give me just a minute; I was just walking Detective Spencer out." I shook his hand, and he held mine longer than any normal casual shake. His gaze never wavered as his eyes sparkled. I slipped my fingers free and gestured Mason past them.

Mason stopped at his car. His glare was aimed above my head. "You need me to stay and deal with them?"

"I can handle them. Mr. Archer is just dropping off a cold case, and Freddie... well, I told you about him. He saved my life. He's not going to hurt me."

"Even so, but you aren't running around chasing criminals anymore. What does he think you need protecting from?" Mason asked, turning his gaze to mine. His clenched jaw eased.

I shrugged. "Who knows, but I'll call you if I need you."

"You do that," Mason announced while cupping my cheek. He lowered his head and gave me the hottest kiss of my life. It may have been for the benefit of the good-looking men standing on the porch, but I'd take it. My eyes were still closed, and my toes were curled when Mason broke the kiss. I sighed in pleasure.

"Be good, Blue."

My eyes slowly slid open. "It's not in my DNA, Detective. Call me when you're back in town."

He glanced up at the porch one last time. "I'll be back in a bit, with that dinner I promised."

I smiled and walked backward toward the porch. I felt like a schoolgirl with her first crush. "I'll make the dessert."

He winked and grinned as he slid into his car.

Chapter 17

I invited both guys inside. I stuck West Archer in the library before taking Freddie into the kitchen.

"Did Moreno send you?" I asked while unwrapping the latest concoction of cookies I'd baked.

"No, but he sends his regards."

"What are you doing here, Freddie?" I walked to the fridge and poured a glass of sweet tea and set it in front of him next to the plate.

"I've already told you. I'm your new bodyguard."

"I wasn't looking for one." I gestured to the cookies.

"Just because you weren't looking for one doesn't mean you don't need one."

I sighed.

"This is a big place you got here."

I glanced at the bag at his feet. "You need somewhere to stay?"

"If I'm going to guard you, it makes sense I'm close by."

I shook my head and tossed up my hands. "Faraday will be staying here soon."

"Even more reason you need me here. Don't worry. I'll pay rent for one of your rooms. Trust me, you need me, Blue." He glanced around the kitchen, ignoring the cookies I had offered. There was something tense about his posture, the way his gaze was floating across the room.

"I work cold cases, Freddie. I'm not going to do any more active ones."

"You need me, and I need you." He glanced in the corner where my Grammy was standing. "She told me you do."

My mouth parted. "You can see her?"

He rubbed at his neck. "Yep. I'm going to teach you how to defend yourself, and you're going to teach me how to make them go away."

"Fine." I gestured toward the stairs. "You can have the room at the end of the hall on the second floor."

Freddie tossed the bag strap over his shoulder, then grabbed the plate of cookies and tea before he disappeared up the back stairs.

I left the kitchen to deal with the stranger in the library. I walked into find him standing behind my desk. "Well, West Archer, did you bring the package?"

"No, but I have it in a safe place," he answered. "I wanted to introduce myself first."

"Are you with the FBI?" I asked.

He grinned. "I can assure you I am not part of your government."

Perfect. Maybe having Freddie in the house wasn't such a bad idea.

"I'm afraid I don't let people watch me when I work."

"You'll have to make an exception."

I crossed my arms over my chest. "What's the case?"

He pulled a document out of the inside pocket of his suit and handed it to me. The envelope had my name written it on. I slipped the document free. It was a non-disclosure agreement. "Both of our governments insist that you sign that document before I can disclose any information. It's a formality."

I ran my fingertip over the embossed U.S. and very British-looking seal insignia. "It's an international case?"

I glanced up to find he'd folded his hands and didn't have any plan on answering my question.

"Okay, then." I scanned the document and grabbed a pen from my desk, scribbling my name at the bottom. I waited impatiently as he slipped it back inside the envelope and returned it to his suit pocket.

"The Wellington Diamond."

I think my heart momentarily stopped. I remember hearing about that case, but it was nothing more than a fairy tale. A sacred diamond that had been given to a famous actress by the very "married" Prince of Wellington. I slowly had to sit down before my legs gave out beneath me. "It's true?"

"Most of it." He grinned. "Do I have your interest now?"

I nodded, unable to form words. This would be the case of a lifetime, one that I'd grown up all my life intrigued by. Hell yes, he had my interest. "When can we start?"

His mischievous smile grew as he met my gaze. "I have a few things to wrap up, and then I'll be back in a few weeks."

I let out a shaky breath. "Okay."

"I look forward to seeing how far we take this."

"Me too." I rose from my chair and walked him to the door.

He stepped outside and turned at the last minute. "I hope you're ready for one hell of a ride, Cree Blue." His gaze lingered on my lips. "I know I am."

The End.

DEAD WRONG

Thank you for spending time with Cree and her crew. There are several books coming soon in this series. If you enjoyed the book please consider leaving a review.

Next up is <u>Deadly Vows</u> Release Date October 23, 2017

Psychic Cree Blue is working on a cold case where the motives and suspects multiply like the spices in her cooking. When Davina Richards went missing the day before her wedding, people assumed she was a runaway bride. Only Cree knows differently. This bride skipped being a missing person and landed smack-dab in the dead zone. One thing is certain; the ghostly apparition is out to set the record straight and needs Cree's help.

Chock full of more guarded mystery than the Colonel's secret recipe, the case of the deadly vows is Cree's toughest cold case yet. She'll have to rely on more than her intuition and insight if she wants to solve this mystery.

It's no longer a question of who wanted to silence the bride; it's a matter of which one pulled the trigger.

DEAD WRONG

Text KATE to 313131 and get a text message on release dates!

Sign up for her newsletters at www.kateallenton.com

Other Books by Kate Allenton

Suggested Reading Order

BENNETT SISTERS BOX SET (Books 1-4 in one bundle, 1218 pages)

BENNETT SISTERS BOX SET VOLUME 2 (Books 5-7 in one bundle, 517 pages}

INTUITION (Book 1)

TOUCH OF FATE (Book 2)

MIND PLAY (Book 3)

THE RECKONING (Book 4)

REDEMPTION (Book 5)

CHANCE ENCOUNTERS (Book 6)

DESTINED HEARTS (Book 7)

PHANTOM PROTECTORS BOX SET (Books 1-4 in one bundle, 964 pages)

RECKLESS ABANDON (Book 1)

BETRAYAL (Book 2)

UNTAMED (Book 3)

GUIDED LOYALTY (Book 4)

CARRINGTON-HILL INVESTIGATIONS

DECEPTION (Book 1)

DEADLY DESIRE (Book 2)

DEAD WRONG

SHIFTER PARADISE BOX SET
NOT MY SHIFTER/ SINFULLY CURSED

KARMA

SOPHIE MASTERSON SERIES/ DIXON SECURITY
LIFTING THE VEIL (Book 1)
BEYOND THE VEIL (Book 2)
VEILED INTENTIONS (Book 3)
VEILED THREATS (Book 4)

THE LOVE FAMILY SERIES
SKYLAR (BOOK1)
DECLAN (BOOK 2)
FLYNN (BOOK 3)
REED (BOOK 4)
LANDON (BOOK 5)
ALEXIS (BOOK 6)
GABE (BOOK 7)
JACKSON (BOOK 8)

LINKED INC.
DEADLY INTENT (BOOK 1)
PSYCHIC LINK (BOOK 2)
PSYCHIC CHARM (BOOK 3)
PSYCHIC GAMES (BOOK 4)
DEADLY DREAMS (BOOK 5)

CREE BLUE PSYCHIC EYE
<u>DEAD WRONG</u> (BOOK 1)
<u>DEADLY VOWS</u> (BOOK 2)
DEADLY HEIST (BOOK 3- COMING DEC 2018)

<u>HELL BOUND</u>
<u>MYSTIC TIDES BOX SET</u>
<u>MYSTIC LUCK BOX SET</u>
<u>MAID OF HONOR</u>
<u>HARD SHIFT</u>

About the Author

Kate has lived in Florida for most of her entire life. She enjoys a quiet life with her husband, Michael and two kids.

Kate has pulled all-nighters finishing her favorite books and also writing them. She says she'll sleep when she's dead or when her muse stops singing off key.

She loves creating worlds full of suspense, secrets, hunky men, kick ass heroines, steamy sex and oh yeah the love of a lifetime. Not to mention an occasional ghost and other supernatural talents thrown into the mix.
Sign up for her newsletters HERE
She loves to hear from her readers by email at KateAllenton@hotmail.com, on Twitter@KateAllenton, and on Facebook at facebook.com/kateallenton.1
Visit her website at www.kateallenton.com
Visit Coastal Escape Publishing's website at www.coastalescapepublishing.com

19378318R00110

Made in the USA
Middletown, DE
05 December 2018